# TO ENSNARE A PRINCE

# THE FOUR KINGDOMS AND BEYOND

## THE FOUR KINGDOMS

The Princess Companion: A Retelling of The Princess and the Pea (Book One)

The Princess Fugitive: A Reimagining of Little Red Riding Hood (Book Two)

The Coronation Ball: A Four Kingdoms Cinderella Novelette

Happily Every Afters: A Reimagining of Snow White and Rose Red (Novella)

The Princess Pact: A Twist on Rumpelstiltskin (Book Three)

A Midwinter's Wedding: A Retelling of The Frog Prince (Novella)

The Princess Game: A Reimagining of Sleeping Beauty (Book Four)

The Princess Search: A Retelling of The Ugly Duckling (Book Five)

## BEYOND THE FOUR KINGDOMS

A Dance of Silver and Shadow: A Retelling of The Twelve Dancing Princesses (Book One)

A Tale of Beauty and Beast: A Retelling of Beauty and the Beast (Book Two)

A Crown of Snow and Ice: A Retelling of The Snow Queen (Book Three)

A Dream of Ebony and White: A Retelling of Snow White (Book Four)

A Captive of Wing and Feather: A Retelling of Swan Lake (Book Five)

A Princess of Wind and Wave: A Retelling of The Little Mermaid (Book Six)

## RETURN TO THE FOUR KINGDOMS

The Secret Princess: A Retelling of The Goose Girl (Book One)

The Mystery Princess: A Retelling of Cinderella (Book Two)

The Desert Princess: A Retelling of Aladdin (Book Three)

The Golden Princess: A Retelling of Ali Baba and the Forty Thieves (Book Four)

The Rogue Princess: A Retelling of Puss in Boots (Book Five)

The Abandoned Princess: A Retelling of Rapunzel (Book Six)

## FOUR KINGDOMS DUOLOGY

To Ride the Wind: A Retelling of East of the Sun and West of the Moon (Book One)

To Steal the Sun: A Retelling of East of the Sun and West of the Moon (Book Two)

## FOUR KINGDOMS FAIRY TALE NOVELLAS

To Ensnare a Prince: An Entwined Prince and the Pauper Retelling (Book One)

To Entangle a Heart: An Entwined Prince and the Pauper Retelling (Book Two)

# TO ENSNARE A PRINCE

## AN ENTWINED PRINCE AND THE PAUPER RETELLING

### FOUR KINGDOMS FAIRY TALE NOVELLAS BOOK 1

## MELANIE CELLIER

LUMINANT PUBLICATIONS

*For Keryn,*
*a faithful and steadfast friend*

Four Kingdoms
GREENHOW
NORTHGATE
Northhelm
RANGMEROS
Rangmere
Arcadia
BORDER GRASSLAND
HEVER CASTLE
ARCADIE
Kuralan
The Great Desert
KAREMA
MIADUS
LANARE
Lanovere
SERRALA
CATALIF
INVERNE
Ardasira
BANISHMENT
ISLAND

# CHAPTER 1

*N*atalie's heart lifted with every bounce of the carriage. Not that there were many of those—it was the most luxurious carriage she'd ever ridden in.

"I suppose this seems slow to you," her companion said, glancing out the window at the spring sunshine bathing the passing fields, her face at odds with the cheery scene.

Natalie examined the face of the golden-haired princess across from her and concluded that she looked concerned. Curiosity instantly flooded her. They were heading to a royal court for a social visit which was sure to mean a succession of parties, balls, picnics, and every other delightful diversion. What possible cause did Princess Rose have for despondency?

"A carriage is considerably slower than riding the wind," Natalie acknowledged, her eyes on the princess rather than the view. "But it's also a lot less cold."

A surprised chuckle escaped Rose. "I never thought about that aspect. Why is nothing ever as delightful as it looks from the outside?"

Natalie's brows rose. "Really? So far this experience is proving far better than I hoped."

She let her attention wander out the window, her mouth curving upward again. After three long years of waiting, she was finally on her way to Lanover and Prince Leo.

"Better?" Rose's doubtful tone sent Natalie's eyes snapping back to the other girl.

When Natalie had arrived in Arcadia, traveling in style on the wind with Queen Gwendolyn of the mountain kingdom, she had ostensibly come to visit Charlotte. And Natalie had been genuinely pleased to see her old friend—now officially crown princess of Arcadia thanks to her marriage to Rose's older brother. But Natalie's focus had been finding a means to continue on to Lanover.

Her parents had promised her a visit to Arcadia when she turned eighteen, but Natalie's true goal had always been Lanover. The discovery that King Max and Queen Alyssa were about to send their daughter on a visit to the southern kingdom had been the best possible news. Natalie had hoped to join a traveling merchant caravan or similar for the journey, but traveling in a royal carriage in company with a princess was a far superior option.

She had been a little surprised at the Arcadian king and queen's ready invitation for their new acquaintance to join their daughter, however, and now she was more curious than ever. Was something going on that Natalie didn't yet understand? At the Arcadian court, Rose had seemed friendly, cheerful, and confident.

Natalie leaned forward.

"Is something wrong?" she asked. "You can tell me, if you like. I'm a very reliable secret-keeper." She gave Rose what she hoped was a confidence-inspiring smile.

Rose smiled back. "Queen Gwendolyn spoke of you in glowing terms, so I'm sure you're very reliable."

Natalie wrinkled her nose. She didn't want to be *unreliable*, of course, but of all the possible traits to be known by…

Rose must have understood the emotion behind Natalie's expression because she laughed. "Queen Gwendolyn was telling me about the rebellion three years ago when your kingdom overthrew the usurper queen and restored Queen Gwendolyn to the throne. She said you played a crucial role. Is that true? You must have only been fourteen or fifteen back then. Did they really let you help?"

Natalie sighed. "Back then they did." Her brows drew together. "Not with any enthusiasm, mind you. They just didn't have a lot of options." Resentment flooded her thoughts. "I was the one to seek out the rebels at court in the first place, and yet they still kept trying to cut me out of everything!"

"Surely they only wanted to protect you?" Rose protested.

Natalie shrugged. "Of course. They insisted on seeing me as a child. But I wasn't the one constantly getting myself injured or captured or…" She shook herself, pushing aside the old injustices. "Never mind all that."

If she kept talking, she would end up having to explain about her brother, and she had no desire for Baden to ruin her mood. He had done enough damage already.

Rose also sank back against her seat, her own brief animation fading. As her earlier despondence returned, she sighed.

"The last time something that exciting happened in Arcadia, I was only six years old, and no one told me anything until it was all over."

Natalie gave her a sympathetic look. No one could understand Rose's frustration better than Natalie. Ever since the end of the rebellion, her parents had relentlessly shut her out of all excitement, despite Natalie being sixteen, not six. They hadn't cared that, after taking part in such dramatic events, it had been torturous to find herself shut out of the court and everything that mattered.

But Rose already had what Natalie wanted—she was a royal, guaranteed to remain in the middle of everything that was happening across the kingdoms. And she was even on her first solo royal visit. If her issue was that she was longing for adventure, shouldn't she be more excited?

Rose's parents had even acquiesced with her request that they not send any older courtiers with her. Other than Natalie, only Rose's maids followed in the second carriage. Even the troop of guards who rode beside them would turn back once they reached the border, handing responsibility for the carriage to the Lanoverian honor guard who would be waiting there.

*Which,* Natalie reflected, *might be the reason the king and queen had been so pleased to discover a companion their daughter would accept.*

But it didn't give any insight into the princess's attitude. She had been allowed to have her own way with the visit to Lanover, so what was left to distress her?

Rose looked at her, hesitated, and then spoke, the words bursting out of her. "When my brother turned eighteen, he went traveling alone and got into all sorts of trouble. We didn't even know if he was alive! But I've always been a dutiful, obedient, perfect princess."

"Is that a problem?" Natalie asked cautiously.

"Even I have my limits!" Rose declared. "I'm not obediently trotting off to Lanover to marry Crown Prince Leo like everyone wants!"

"That's good," Natalie said matter-of-factly, "since I intend to marry him myself."

Rose blinked at her. "*You're* going to marry Prince Leo?"

Natalie cocked her head to the side. "Why not? Your mother was a commoner before she married your father, and so was Charlotte before she married your brother."

"I didn't mean…" Rose shook her head. "I just had no idea you'd been to Lanover before! Or has Leo visited the mountain kingdom? I had no idea he was already in love." She looked lighter and happier than she had moments before.

"Oh, Leo and I have never met," Natalie said. "But I'm going to be a queen one day, like Charlotte."

During the rebellion, Natalie had been just as central to what was happening as Charlotte, and only a few short years lay between their ages. But no one had told Charlotte to forget about rebellions and go back to a boring, ordinary life. Why was that? Because Charlotte had become a royal. She had made herself too important to be shut out.

And now that Natalie was eighteen and no longer confined to the mountain kingdom, there was no reason she couldn't do the same. Her spirits rose. If everyone was busy planning a wedding between Rose and Leo, then they obviously weren't planning one between him and anyone else. And if Rose didn't want Leo for herself, after all, then Natalie's path was clear.

Across from her, Rose had stiffened. "Are you serious? You asked to accompany me to Lanover because you want to trick Prince Leo into marrying you so that you can become a princess?"

"A queen," Natalie corrected her absentmindedly, before realizing the depths of the other girl's indignation.

"That's outrageous!" Rose cried. "I would never have done as you asked and requested to have you accompany me if I'd known you were going to Lanover with...with mercenary motives! I may not have met Prince Leo before, but I won't let you trick him!"

"Who said anything about tricking!?" Natalie tried to keep a lid on her temper. It had gotten her into trouble before, since it usually burned hot, if short. "It's not as if I have an enchanted object on hand to force him to fall in love with me. I'm just giving him the chance to get to know me. If he falls in love with me on his own, then fair's fair. I don't see what's wrong with that. And I'm not mercenary at all. I have no particular interest in gold. I didn't pick Lanover because it's the wealthiest kingdom. It was the only one that had a crown prince the right age."

"The only one that..." Rose sputtered, her sentence trailing off and her eyes enormous as she regarded Natalie.

"What's the matter now?" Natalie asked, indignant.

Rose's condemnation abruptly melted into a fit of the giggles. "You...You're..." She couldn't get a full sentence out, so Natalie was forced to watch her in silence as she got herself under control.

"You might not be mercenary for money, but you're certainly pursuing Prince Leo for his rank," she finally said, when she could speak steadily again. "You can't deny that."

Natalie considered the matter. "That's true. But it's not as if I want the rank so I can live a rich, easy life, or have people bowing to me all the time."

"Why do you want it, then?" Rose demanded.

"I want to matter," Natalie exclaimed, her earlier resentment sparking a torrent of words. "Or, at least, I want to do things that matter. Is that such a terrible thing? During the rebellion, my actions helped to change everything—not just for me but for my whole kingdom. It was incredible!" She deflated. "But I'm just a commoner girl, so it was easy for them to exile me after their desperate need was over."

"Exile?" Rose stared at her, startled out of her anger. "Queen Gwendolyn brought you to Arcadia herself! She seemed genuinely fond of you."

"It wasn't Gwen who barred me from court," Natalie said, fair as always. "She even argued my case to my parents. But they were convinced that the best thing for me was to go back to an ordinary life and forget about everything that had happened."

She scowled out at the unoffending view.

"Perhaps," Rose said, sounding like she was once again smothering a laugh, "they were concerned about your obsession with becoming royal. Or is that a newer goal?"

Natalie looked across at her, smiling reluctantly. "The idea may have occurred to me back then, yes. But it started as a momentary dream, fueled by beautiful dresses and the excitement of the moment. It was only later that I realized that becoming royal was the only way to ensure no one could shut me out again."

Natalie's declaration that she would marry Prince Leo one day had been the smallest of her parents' reasons for excluding her from court, but Natalie had no desire to explain the largest. She had played no part in her older brother Baden's betrayal, and it was unjust of her parents to punish her for his crimes. He had been truly exiled—banished from the mountain kingdom—and Natalie hadn't seen him in three years. Usually she didn't even like to think about him. He had lost his place in their family when he chose to turn against them all.

But her parents had been convinced that Natalie's presence at court was an unwelcome reminder of her brother's role in the rebellion. Even though Natalie had successfully completed the task assigned to the two of them on her own —assembling the crucial assistance that had turned the tide —she couldn't escape the shadow of her brother's actions.

In fairness, her parents had been seeking to protect her as much as to protect their family's position at court. They didn't want her exposed to the vitriol of the court in Baden's place. Not everyone had felt that banishment was sufficient punishment for a traitor.

But whatever her parents' intentions, their actions had sentenced Natalie to three endless, tedious years of watching the happenings of the kingdom from afar. And if she hadn't fled the mountains, she might still be in that position despite having turned eighteen. Gwen viewed Natalie with affection, but she had already assembled her court, and there was no empty place for Natalie to fill.

But Lanover was different. They had yet to fill the position of crown princess, and there was no reason Natalie shouldn't be the one to step into that role. In Lanover, she could make a place for herself—a place that would always be at the center of everything that mattered.

"There must have been a lot of work needed to rebuild the mountain kingdom after the old queen's brutal rule," Rose said, her tone sympathetic. "I can understand why it was hard to be excluded from that after being central to the rebellion. But that's hardly poor Prince Leo's fault!"

"You say that as if I intend to mistreat him!" Natalie protested. "I have every intention of being a delightful wife. You're supposed to love someone for who they are, and Prince Leo's rank is an integral part of who he is—as well as his future. It would be more of a disaster for him to marry someone unsuited or unwilling to one day be queen than to marry someone who wants that role. His place in the royal family is his whole future." She regarded Rose curiously. "Wouldn't you consider your rank to be an integral part of you?"

"Yes, I suppose so," Rose murmured, not meeting Natalie's eyes.

"Exactly," Natalie said, satisfied. "How many girls throughout history have taken one look at a good-looking young man and decided on the spot to fall in love with him? I don't see how this is any different."

"I suppose it's true that people do that." Rose sounded unconvinced. "But how many of them delude themselves in the process, only to rue that decision later? What if you don't actually like Prince Leo when you meet him?"

Natalie scoffed at that possibility. "The chances of that

seem small. He's sure to be good-looking for a start—the Lanoverian royal family is famed for their beauty. And aren't princes trained to be both charming and responsible? I'm sure he'll be delightful."

"But what if he's arrogant and entitled? He is a crown prince, after all."

"So is your brother," Natalie countered, naming the only other crown prince she'd ever met. "And he's never seemed arrogant. From what I've seen, he's kind, charming, and honorable. I'm sure Leo will be the same."

"Don't tell me you have a misguided affection for Harry!" Rose sounded horrified, and Natalie reciprocated the feeling.

"For Prince Henry? No! He's married! And too old, besides. Leo, on the other hand, is only a year or so older than me." Her voice turned dreamy. "It's perfect."

"But what if you don't like him?" Rose asked, apparently unwilling to enter into Natalie's delight. "What if he laughs at all the wrong things, and you find everything he says boring?"

Natalie couldn't help picturing the awful possibility. The Lanoverian royal family were supposed to be both delightful and intelligent, but every family had an odd one out.

"Then it will all have been for nothing," she said in a small voice.

But she couldn't believe it was true. It couldn't be!

"But I'm sure he'll be perfectly charming!" She spoke the words with conviction, as if she could make them true with her determination.

"Even if you do fall in love with him, what if he doesn't

fall in love with you?" Rose watched her with narrowed eyes. "You won't be the first girl to show interest in him."

"But none of those girls are me." How many of them had taken down a monarchy at fourteen? Natalie had been called plenty of things in her eighteen years, but no one had ever said she was boring.

"I suppose there isn't anything wrong with you making the attempt," Rose finally conceded. "As long as you won't pursue a match unless there turn out to be real feelings on both sides." She grimaced. "That's what my parents are hoping will happen with me, after all. It's almost exactly the same, in fact."

"You see!" Natalie cried, triumphant. Now Rose was understanding. "Far too many people fail at what they want in life because they don't make the effort to go out and get it. Like in my kingdom. Everyone suffered under that usurper for far too long because all the adults dithered instead of taking back the kingdom."

"You say it like it's that easy!" Rose exclaimed.

Natalie shrugged. "I never said it was easy. But if you truly want something, you have to be prepared to sacrifice for it. And dithering in the meantime won't get you anywhere." She made a scornful sound in her throat.

"So what's your plan?" Rose asked, finally shedding the last signs of condemnation.

"I'll have to see the lay of the land first." Natalie wished she had a better answer, but despite the many hours she'd spent thinking about the future, it was hard to make plans when she knew so little about the regular operation of the Lanoverian court. "I expect my biggest issue will be getting enough time with Prince Leo. He may be closely guarded."

She stared into the distance as she pictured the potential obstacles.

"Whereas I, on the other hand…" Rose sighed.

But a moment later, her whole demeanor changed. She leaned toward Natalie, her eyes alight. "What if we swapped?"

# CHAPTER 2

"Swapped?" Natalie tried to make sense of the suggestion. "What do you mean?"

"Just for the first few days. As a...a laugh—a prank. That's what we'll tell the others when we switch back anyway. But even if we only keep it up for a few days, it will give you the chance to spend some initial time with Leo. If you truly do like each other, everything else aside, then he won't mind when you turn out not to be a princess after all. And if he does mind, then the feelings weren't real. You can treat it as a test." She gave Natalie a stern look. "And if he has no real feelings for you, you have to promise you'll let the whole idea of marrying him go."

"You mean we should switch places? That I would arrive in Lanover as Princess Rose and you as Natalie?" The mischief of it appealed to Natalie even before she considered the potential benefits. "But how could that ever work? We don't look anything alike!"

"That doesn't matter." Rose grew more and more animated as she explained her idea. "My maids are loyal to me and will stay quiet if I ask it. And I've never met Prince Leo, only his sister, Princess Beatrice. King Frederic and Queen Evangeline have visited the Arcadian court with Beatrice, but none of them are going to be at the Lanoverian court when we arrive. Now that King Leonardo and Queen Viktoria have stepped down, and Leo's parents have been crowned king and queen, all four of them are going on a tour of the kingdom to ease the transition. Almost all the senior court are going too, as well as Princess Beatrice and her cousins, Princess Violet and Princess Iris. Only the prince is being left behind. From what my parents said, I think it's a test of sorts—to see how Prince Leo performs in their absence, now that he's officially crown prince. It's why my parents agreed to send me alone. It will only be a few younger members of court at the Lanoverian palace for the next few weeks."

"Only young people? Are you sure?" Natalie's mind raced with the possibilities.

Rose's plan would give Natalie direct and easy access to Leo—far easier than she had dared dream. Of course, he might be offended at finding himself fooled, but it wasn't as if they were planning to keep the ruse going. Once Natalie had been given the chance to actually connect with him, she would tell him the truth readily. She wasn't foolish enough to let things get serious while he thought she was royalty.

"I heard the Duke of Sessily will be staying—*to keep a discreet eye on the young prince.*" Rose said the words as if she was repeating something she had heard someone else say. "But I've never met him either, only his mother the

Dowager Duchess—and despite her age, she'll be going with the tour."

"I thought you weren't willing to trick Prince Leo," Natalie teased, her excitement growing stronger by the minute.

"This is different," Rose said with a royal dignity she seemed able to put on at will. "While I'm sure he doesn't want to be courted only for his rank, neither do I. Fooling him into calling us the wrong names for a few days is hardly a trick of any consequence." She gave Natalie a significant look. "It's not at all the same as fooling him into committing his life to someone whose only interest in him is acquiring his rank."

Natalie laughed. "From everything I've heard, it's exactly the sort of prank that would appeal to Prince Leo. According to the rumors, he and his cousin, Prince Luca, spent their entire childhood getting into mischief. So he can hardly get angry at us for doing something similar ourselves."

"If he's the sort of person who can't take what he himself dishes out, then neither of us should marry him, prince or not," Rose said softly but with determination. "So it really is a test of sorts." She gave Natalie another look. "And you do need a test, given the danger of deciding who you're going to fall in love with before you know anything about them as a person."

"That seems fair," Natalie said. "But I'm sure he'll pass the test. I don't expect to have any problem caring for Leo the person."

Rose gave a soft sigh, her mood falling inexplicably, and Natalie's earlier curiosity was roused.

"Why are you so set against him, anyway?" she asked. "Given everything we've heard about Prince Leo and the whole Lanoverian family, he's likely to be an easy person to fall in love with. Not that I'm not grateful," she hastened to add. "I wouldn't want us to be in competition."

"I just want to make my own choice." Rose looked down. "But I'm afraid of…"

Her usual poise had disappeared completely, and Natalie's curiosity gave way to something sharper and more intense. She leaned forward.

"You're afraid? Has someone been threatening you?" She sucked in a breath. "Have they hurt you?" All thoughts of her own mission were forgotten, burned away in the fire of her wrath. Who could want to hurt someone as genuinely sweet as Rose seemed to be? And a princess, besides! They must be a monster.

"Is that why you've been so on edge?" she demanded. "Is that why you want to switch places?" She didn't wait for an answer. "Because if so, forget a short-term ruse. We can turn the carriage around right now, and I'll sort the villain out before we go a mile further."

"Would you really?" Rose goggled at her. "And what if it's my parents, the king and queen?"

Natalie frowned. King Max and Queen Alyssa had seemed like genuine, compassionate people to her, but Natalie had misread people before.

She reached across the gap between the carriage seats and took Rose's hand in a firm grip. "Don't worry. We'll find a way. You can count me as a friend, no matter what." She drew a deep breath. "I've helped bring down a ruler before."

"I can see how. You really don't let anything overwhelm you, do you?" Rose squeezed her hand before withdrawing from her grip and laughing. "But don't worry. No one is abusing me. When I said I was afraid, I meant I was afraid of disappointing my parents. If I turned Leo down, they would never complain to me, but I know an alliance with Lanover would help Arcadia. Not that my parents would want me to sacrifice my happiness, but…well…as you said, I suppose they're thinking that Leo would be an easy person to love."

"But you don't want to love him." Natalie relaxed back into her seat, her blood pressure returning to normal now that the apparent danger was allayed.

Rose just shrugged and looked out the window. Natalie continued to watch her, but the silence didn't tempt Rose into confessing whatever thoughts filled her mind.

"So we're really going to do this?" Natalie eventually asked, some of her earlier excitement rekindling.

Rose smiled at her and nodded decisively. "I'll talk to my maids at the next rest stop. They'll insist one of them stays with me in whatever room you're assigned, but it will be simple enough for you to say that you've instructed one of your maids to take care of your friend. Since mother insisted I bring *four*, no one will wonder about that."

Natalie reached out her hand again, and this time, Rose shook it, the two girls grinning at each other. Natalie had liked Rose from the beginning and been grateful to her, but she was now certain they had the potential to be firm friends.

"You'd better tell me more about your family and Arcadia," Natalie said. "So I don't say the wrong thing and expose our switch too early."

"Yes, of course," Rose said. "We've got plenty of time while we're traveling. And you can tell me about the mountain kingdom. I've been wanting to hear more about it and about your rebellion."

Natalie nodded agreement, but her mind was still on the practicalities. "At least we won't have to worry about switching clothes. Queen Gwen insisted on gifting me a magnificent new wardrobe for my eighteenth birthday since she knew I was coming to visit your court."

"You're taller than me, so that would never work anyway," Rose said, assessing Natalie with a considered gaze. "Oh, and if anyone tries to talk policy with you, deflect the conversation. And if you get any notes for me, make sure you pass them on. I don't want our little game to turn into an international incident."

Natalie grinned. "I'm excellent at deflecting conversations when they turn to topics I don't want to talk about."

Rose laughed. "Why do I not find that hard to believe? Do you ever do anything you don't want to do?"

Natalie sighed. "I've been doing hardly anything else for the last three years. But hopefully that will change soon, once I'm a princess."

Rose eyed her with a doubtful expression. "Perhaps..." she said slowly, but Natalie wasn't really listening. She was too busy imagining her glowing future.

# CHAPTER 3

When they crossed the southern border of Arcadia, the guards changed, and the maids started obediently addressing Natalie as Your Highness. Hearing it the first few times was a thrill, but when they approached Lanare, the capital of Lanover, even Natalie's confidence wavered.

What had seemed like an excellent lark when the two were alone in the middle of endless fields looked a little different in the bright sun of an unfamiliar city. Everything around her looked foreign—different from both her home kingdom and from Arcadia—reminding her that she might be out of her depth. Even the air held an unfamiliar hint of moisture, although Natalie had heard it got far worse in the south of the kingdom.

But Natalie had been making her plans for too long to shrink away from them at the first hint of uncertainty. She refused to go meekly home to the mountains and a life of irrelevance and boredom. Lanover might look unfamiliar now, but she would grow accustomed to it soon enough.

Natalie leaned out of the carriage to drink in her new home. The city was an unexpected combination of dusty, understated sandstone and bright, vibrant plant life. Everywhere she looked she saw flowers, each of them a splash of color against the reddish stone.

A small but insistent hand gave her a sharp tug. Unbalanced, she fell back inside the carriage. Natalie glared at Rose, but the princess was glaring back.

"You're a princess now, remember!" she hissed. "And princesses on visits of state don't hang out carriage windows. You promised to behave in a way that wouldn't bring Arcadia into disrepute!"

Natalie bit her lip and sat meekly back on the carriage seat. Maybe the task was going to prove more difficult than she'd blithely assumed.

For a moment, she thought Rose was second-guessing the entire charade, but as soon as Natalie sat down, a grin spread over Rose's face.

"I, however, am not currently a princess." She promptly stuck her own head out the window Natalie had just vacated.

Natalie snorted, but something about Rose's obvious joy was infectious, and she settled for gazing avidly out the other window. At least princesses were allowed to look—as long as they kept themselves decorously inside the carriage.

They had entered Lanover from the north, but the hills above the capital necessitated a roundabout route into the city itself. As a result, they rolled northward through the streets of the sprawling, single-storied city, approaching the first of those hills.

Atop it sat the palace, facing south. Natalie had already seen the bare hills and treacherous slopes that guarded the rear of the palace, but before it spread the glorious vista of the large city, unimpeded by high walls. Natalie had spent time in two palaces in her eighteen years, and neither of them had prepared her for the sight of the Lanoverian royal residence.

There was no sign of polished white marble or rugged gray stone—just the same red of the city's sandstone. Neither were there intimidating turrets or soaring spires. The palace was only a single story like the rest of the city, standing out due to its size and location—and the vast gardens that completely encircled it. It was by far the most welcoming palace Natalie had ever seen, and she loved it instantly.

"It's beautiful!" she breathed.

"It is," Rose murmured, pulling back to sit sedately in the carriage once more. "It's nothing like home but it's… inviting."

"Yes, that's just the word for it," Natalie agreed enthusiastically.

But while Natalie's spirits were rising, Rose's seemed to be falling. When the princess caught Natalie's worried gaze, however, she smiled.

"Don't worry, I'm not having second thoughts. You'll have your chance to be a princess for a few days."

Natalie grinned, her eyes drawn back to the approaching palace. As their carriage rolled through the elaborate gardens, she itched to get out and walk. Everywhere she looked, unfamiliar plants and flowers caught her eye. But she remained in her seat until they reached the front of the palace, and a footman appeared to help her alight.

Rose followed her out, also politely assisted by the footman, but she immediately melted away from Natalie's side. Natalie had expected them to face the palace together, but instead she stood alone to greet the people who had appeared in response to the carriage's arrival.

The first to step out was a tall young man with the golden skin and dark hair of the Lanoverian royal family. An understated golden circlet rested in his generous dark hair, similar to the one that Natalie now wore nestled in her own elaborate arrangement of hair. But her eyes were drawn more to the prince's broad shoulders, and the sight of his handsome features made her pulse quicken. He was even more attractive than she had dared hope. Loving him was going to be no difficulty at all.

Natalie's lips curved upward, but before she could drop into a curtsy in the manner Rose had taught her, a second young man stepped around the first and approached her with an easy smile. He also wore a circlet, this one more elaborate than the other, and he had the same coloring.

Natalie froze, her eyes flickering between the two men before settling on the second. From his crown alone she recognized her mistake. This was the crown prince, not the first man.

His smile was still in place as he gave a shallow bow. She responded automatically with the practiced curtsy, allowing him to take her hand and bend his head over it. But the moment of her first meeting with Prince Leo—which should have been magical—had somehow been stripped of its spark.

She tried to ignore the first man who was watching her with something suspiciously like laughter in his eyes as she forced herself to focus on the words of the one holding her hand.

"Welcome to Lanover, Princess Rose. It's an honor to have you here. I am Crown Prince Leo, and I will be your host on behalf of my parents."

"Thank you, Your Highness," Natalie said, her focus regained. "I'm glad to be here."

She peeped up at him through her lashes, hoping she looked less avidly curious than she felt. Leo was just as uncommonly handsome as the first man—who must surely be his cousin—and there was no reason for her to feel disappointed at the momentary mistake.

"Please, call me Leo," he said with a disarming smile, and she instinctively smiled back.

"In that case, you must call me Rose," she said. Sudden inspiration struck, and she added, "Or better yet, call me Lila, since I can already tell that we're going to be friends." She gave him her warmest smile, and he tucked her hand into his arm, turning them both toward the palace doors.

"Lila? Is that what your friends call you?"

"It's been my pet name since childhood," she said. "It means *little flower.*"

It only meant that in the mountain kingdom, but she was trusting no one in Lanover would know that. She snuck a look at the real Rose—who was standing with a clump of people to one side of the carriage—and received a grin of encouragement.

"I hope you don't mind, but I brought a friend with me." Natalie gestured toward Rose. "Her name is Natalie, and she's from the mountain kingdom. She's on a tour of the Four Kingdoms, so I insisted she join me on my journey to Lanover. I hope you might have a room for her."

She peeked up at Leo again, but he was looking toward Rose, his gaze lingering in a way that made Natalie nervous. Did he recognize the real princess? If he'd seen a portrait of the Arcadian royal family, their charade would be over before it began.

But a moment later he looked back down at her, a smile still locked on his face, and no words of denunciation on his lips.

"Of course. Any friend of yours is welcome here. And I confess to great curiosity about the mountain kingdom. I hope to have a chance to talk with Natalie about it at some point."

Something warm blossomed inside Natalie. Perhaps she truly would be welcomed here, even under her own identity.

She almost confessed to the charade on the spot, but the other young man stepped forward at that moment, and the sight of his laughing eyes hardened her resolve. He had caught her brief mistake earlier, and he was laughing at her. She intended to put a stop to that.

"I'm Prince Luca," he said, "son of Prince Cassian and Princess Tillara."

She had been right about his identity. Prince Cassian was the younger brother of the new King Frederic, and his children had been raised in the palace alongside his brother's children. From everything she'd heard, Leo and Luca were more like brothers than cousins.

Prince Luca held out his hand, as if he intended to take

hers and press it to his lips as Leo had done. Natalie, buoyed by the feeling of her hand tucked in Leo's strong arm, merely looked at the outheld hand blankly and then back up into his face.

"Oh yes," she said sweetly, giving him her best smile. "I did hear something about a second prince." She held her smile in place, confident in the knowledge she looked better than she ever had before. She looked like a princess.

But Luca remained unabashed, merely putting his empty hand into a pocket and laughing. "Yes, indeed," he said. "I'm not even the spare since that role falls to Leo's sister, Princess Beatrice. So you needn't pay me the least heed."

"Luca," Leo said in a warning tone before glancing in Rose's direction. "Perhaps you could escort Lila's friend inside and see she has everything she needs."

"To hear is to obey," Luca said promptly, but his eyes were now laughing at both of them.

Natalie's furious eyes wanted to follow him as he strolled toward Rose, but she disciplined herself not to turn her head. She refused to give him the satisfaction.

Instead, she turned her attention back to Prince Leo. He was her future, and she wasn't going to allow anything or anyone—however irritating—to distract her from it.

# CHAPTER 4

Natalie flopped back on the enormous bed and gave a delighted sigh. The room that had been assigned to the visiting Arcadian princess was by far the nicest she had ever stayed in. It was almost too big—except for the fact she was sharing it with three other women.

She sat up again and smiled at Hilary, who was unpacking her bags into the ornate wardrobe provided.

"You don't have to do that," she said. "I'm not really Rose."

Hilary didn't pause. "That may be, and I'm not saying I approve of such shenanigans, mind! But if I'm here, I might as well busy my hands as not. Her Majesty insisted on sending four of us, but in truth, we're likely to be sitting on our hands half the day, even with two girls to care for instead of one. It's not as if we'll be expected to perform any excess duties in this place."

"Almost like a holiday, you could say," Donna added, unpacking a small case onto the dressing table.

Cate chuckled. "And I, for one, plan to make the most of it."

"Do you like working for the Arcadians?" Natalie asked, curious as to whether the women would speak freely in the absence of their princess.

"Oh yes, certainly," Donna said without hesitation.

"They treat us fair and pay us well." Hilary put the last piece of clothing away and turned to face the others.

"They've been more than kind to me," Cate added. "Her Majesty was only going to send three maids with Her Highness, but she added me at the last minute because she knew I'd taken a liking to a Lanoverian young man when he traveled through Arcadia recently. He took a temporary job at our palace when we were needing some extra hands, but he left to return home a few months ago, and we've only been able to exchange letters since."

The other two women exchanged amused looks, clearly having heard all about Cate's young man already.

"He works at the palace here now," Cate finished with a flush. "So, as I said, I mean to make the most of my time here."

Natalie raised her eyebrows, startled. "That's very considerate of Queen Alyssa."

"She didn't do it purely from altruism." Hilary nudged Cate. "We all know Her Majesty thinks there's a chance her daughter will be staying here in Lanover. There's nothing she wouldn't do for her girl—including arranging for there to be a friendly face among the maids in her new home."

"Maybe Cate won't be the only one to decide to stay if the princess does." Donna giggled. "I'd always heard the

Lanoverians were a good-looking lot, and so far they haven't disappointed."

Natalie smiled as all three collapsed into giggles. A week earlier, she would have laughed with them and asked them to point out the men they'd noticed. But now she felt removed—unsure if her participation would be welcome while she was playing the role of their princess.

She stood up to leave and then remembered she had nowhere to go. She was already in her room. But so were the three maids. Did princesses always have so little privacy?

She brushed the thought aside and went over to admire the view from the closest window. Her room was located in a prime position with views of not only the palace gardens but the city spread out beyond them. The whole vista was enchanting.

Her awkwardness lifted, her thoughts turning to the welcome reception Leo had mentioned. She needed to make sure she looked just right—like a princess. She had only a short window to make an initial impression on him, and she wanted to take his breath away.

Thankfully her gowns left nothing to be desired. Gwen had gifted them to her with the hope that once she had the wardrobe of a princess, she would stop strategizing to actually become one. But Natalie had never been one to settle for half measures. And it had been a long time since dresses were her primary reason for wanting to become a queen.

She chose a particularly flattering gown that was a perfect mix between formal and relaxed. All three maids broke off their conversation to approve her choice and help her prepare for the evening. As long as she was playing the role of the Arcadian princess, they were committed to ensuring she didn't embarrass their kingdom with her appearance.

Natalie had spent the last year learning how to put her own hair up into formal arrangements, but it was much easier to sit back and allow Donna to do it. And when she finally sailed out of the room, the last pieces of Natalie's confidence had returned.

A footman waited respectfully in the corridor outside, ready to lead her to the reception room where the event was being held. Natalie followed him in silence, wondering if she might possibly be dreaming. Could it really all be this easy?

The footman paused inside the door of the reception room, giving Natalie a chance to catch her breath as she took in the grand scale of the room and the sea of unfamiliar faces. His ringing voice cut through the conversations, announcing Rose's name and title.

Silence fell as everyone turned to look at her. It held for only a second before fresh conversations broke out in a wave that swept across the room and crashed against her. Natalie smiled in the face of the challenge. She dared any of them to question her royal status.

None of the courtiers who approached her gave any hint of disbelief, however. Instead, they all greeted her with the same empty, impersonal words of greeting. She caught glimpses of curiosity and wary caution beneath some of the masks, but no one broke script with the foreign princess. By the time she'd repeated herself for the thirtieth time, assuring the latest Lanoverian that her travel had gone smoothly, her fixed smile was starting to slip.

A brief break in the endless stream of people gave her the chance to examine the room. She spotted Rose by the refreshment table, her plate piled high and an expression of delight on her face as she bit into a pastry. Rose wasn't being accosted by an endless stream of people who all wanted to say the same inane thing the previous twenty people had said.

Natalie's stomach rumbled, and she took a determined step toward Rose. If anyone tried to intercept her, she'd just have to find a polite way to brush them off. But her steps faltered of their own accord as she caught sight of Leo. He stood against one of the other walls, talking earnestly with the older courtier who'd been introduced on her arrival as the duke of Sessily.

Natalie's stomach gave another soft gurgle, but she shook her head. She couldn't lose focus. She hadn't come to the reception as Rose in order to meet the Lanoverian court. She had come there to spend time with Leo, and instead of thinking about her stomach, she should be focusing on the bigger goal.

She just needed a chance to get to know him. Once she saw the real him, she would feel the spark that had been missing at their meeting. It would certainly not be a hardship to spend time with such a handsome man.

She changed direction, moving toward Leo instead of the refreshment table. He hadn't spotted her yet, but he could hardly rebuff her at a reception held in her honor.

Someone stepped smoothly in front of her, halting her forward progress just before she reached the crown prince.

The unwelcome face grinned down at her, the smile bordering on a smirk.

"Excuse me," she said in the sweetest tones she could manage, her eyes still on Leo as she attempted to sidestep his cousin.

Luca stepped with her, keeping his position between her and the crown prince.

Natalie sighed. "Can I help you, Your Highness?"

"I thought we agreed on first names, Lee-lah," he said, pronouncing her nickname slowly, his mouth seeming to savor each syllable.

She put her hands on her hips. "I remember making that agreement with Leo, Prince Luca, not with you."

"But I came to rescue you." He adopted a hurt expression that didn't reach his laughing eyes. "Surely I deserve some reward."

Natalie raised an eyebrow. "Rescue me from what exactly?"

"Hunger, of course," he replied promptly, gesturing toward the refreshment table. "I saw you eyeing it earlier, so don't tell me you're not hungry."

Natalie sighed. If she tried to deny it, her stomach would probably betray her and give its loudest rumble yet. She hadn't eaten since arriving in the capital, and she was starving.

She sent a final glance toward Leo. But there was little point trying to spend time with him if his cousin was determined to hover at her side, laughing at her the whole time. She would have to find another opportunity.

"Lead on, then, *Luca*," she said in a resigned voice.

Luca offered his arm courteously, but Natalie ignored

it, starting toward the refreshments alone. Luca laughed quietly and caught up in two strides.

When they reached their destination, Natalie gave a quick glance back toward Leo and caught him looking in her direction. But he immediately turned back to the duke, showing no inclination to end his conversation and join them.

A fleeting thought whispered in her brain. *Who exactly had Luca been rescuing?*

She shook it off. Leo and Luca might have run wild in their younger years, but he had grown up now. He wouldn't have been left in charge during the new king and queen's absence unless they judged him sufficiently responsible. There was no way the crown prince was trying to avoid the foreign princess who had just arrived for a diplomatic visit.

Natalie piled her plate high, refusing to dwell on Leo's distance. The food looked too good not to be enjoyed in the moment.

As she turned from the table with a full plate, she was abruptly reminded of Luca's presence. He stood, watching her with an appreciative gleam in his eye while his own plate remained empty.

"It's nice to see that our Lanoverian chefs meet with Arcadian approval," he said.

"That has yet to be seen," Natalie said loftily, fearing that he was once again laughing at her for making a mistake. Were princesses supposed to confine themselves to eating lightly at royal functions? "I haven't tried any of it yet."

Luca laughed. "My apologies for making assumptions."

"Do you do that a lot?" Natalie asked tartly.

Luca's eyes gleamed. "I may have been guilty in the past, but you're already confounding all my assumptions, Princess."

His casual use of the false title sent a pang of discomfort through Natalie, so she turned away without a word and found a nearby seat. He followed her despite her rude departure, his own plate now full.

They ate in silence for several minutes before Natalie gave up her attempts to take only small, occasional bites and dug into the food properly. She didn't like to pander to the second prince's already comfortable ego, but justice prompted her to retract her earlier qualification and compliment the food.

"There's no need to sound so delighted about it," Luca said with a suppressed laugh. "I promise not to take it as a personal compliment, given I had nothing whatsoever to do with either the menu or food preparation."

His words surprised a laugh out of her. Once again, he had seen her too clearly, and she should have been even more annoyed. But somehow, she couldn't muster the feeling this time.

"If nothing else, I'm fair," she said. "No one could find fault with this food."

"You clearly haven't met Puss." Luca gave a private chuckle.

"Puss?" Natalie asked, intrigued in spite of herself.

Luca launched into a string of tales about the talking cat from the Palace of Light who made occasional visits to Lanover. Clearly the mischief-loving princes had delighted in the creature's arrival, while their parents were less enamored by Puss's presence.

The cat's exploits—aided by a young Leo and Luca—were so amusing that she entirely forgot any remaining irritation with the second prince. Before she knew it, she had finished her plate, her stomach too full to allow another bite. At least not while wearing that dress.

Someone called for Luca's attention, and Natalie took the opportunity to slip away. She would use his distraction to seize another chance with Leo.

But the crown prince was no longer talking to the duke, and it took Natalie several minutes to find him. When she did finally locate him, he had Rose stuck in a back corner, trapped in conversation with him.

Natalie grimaced. It was only the first evening, and she was already failing in her half of the arrangement. Rose had given Natalie her position so that Rose wouldn't end up stuck spending all her time with the prince she was determined not to fall in love with.

Natalie started toward them, resolving to rescue Rose and achieve her own purposes at the same time. But she was once again intercepted before she could reach her goal.

"There you are!" Luca exclaimed. "Some of the courtiers are less mobile than others, and I've been tasked with delivering you to them."

"I'm occupied right now." Natalie's short response barely sounded civil, but it did nothing to discourage Luca.

"You don't look occupied." His look of innocence made her want to shake him.

She drew a deep breath and reminded herself that she

was representing Arcadia and Rose. She couldn't slight the courtiers of Lanover, however irritated she was with their second prince.

"Very well," she said through her teeth, giving him a fake smile and forcing herself to accept his arm.

He smiled broadly, and she told herself she was imagining the look of victory in his eyes as he led her toward the other side of the room. But when he began to pay her fulsome compliments, she snapped.

"Stop that!"

"What's the matter?" he asked in a wounded tone. "It's hardly my fault that your beauty lights up the room. Aren't princesses used to compliments?"

Her step faltered, her eyes flying to his, but she couldn't read anything but amusement in his smile. Had his choice of words been mere chance?

She needed to get a handle on herself. She would have plenty of future opportunities to talk to Leo. For now, she needed to focus on allaying any suspicion.

She forced her face into a more natural smile. "Compliments are one thing, flattery is another. I don't appreciate the latter."

Luca's grin turned a little wicked. "Then you needn't worry, Lila. I meant every word, I assure you. You're a breath of fresh air here."

She gazed at him, her surprise turning to wrath as he extricated himself from her light grasp and disappeared into the crowd with a wave and a wink. She slowly turned to face a clump of elderly courtiers, all of whom were regarding her avidly. Had he truly just fled without even performing introductions?

The babble of voices soon proved his services weren't necessary, and Natalie gave up any hope of keeping all the names and titles straight. They soon explained that they were all too old to go traipsing around the kingdom on tour, which explained their presence at an event almost entirely dominated by young people.

"We don't intend to run ourselves ragged all spring like you young people," one of the women informed her. "But of course we had to come tonight to at least see King Maximilian's youngest for ourselves."

Her words launched a series of reminiscences as the group remembered all the times each of them had seen her supposed parents or grandparents in the past. It took nearly an hour, and Natalie's cheeks were strained from smiling by the end. Natalie herself had remained as silent as possible—a feat she usually found difficult. But her current companions clearly had far more familiarity with the Arcadian royal family than any of the younger courtiers, and she was desperately conscious of the risk of saying something that would give away their charade.

By the time she finally escaped, she had a headache, and she could see no sign of Rose, Leo, or even Luca.

She ground her teeth together as she left the event, wishing cold morning chocolate and holes in his socks on Luca. He deserved it after abandoning her like that.

She stormed through the corridors toward her room, relieved to find she remembered the route. The more she thought about it, the more certain she was that Luca had been playing with her all evening.

But why? What had motivated the prince to treat her

that way when he thought she was Princess Rose? Did he truly suspect their switch?

The idea made her hot and uncomfortable, and she knew her own guilty awareness put her at a disadvantage against him. How could she hold her own against the infuriating man when she had to maintain a façade?

And what had that façade gained her, anyway? She hadn't gotten near Leo all night.

She would go to Rose in the morning and tell her she wanted to switch back immediately. Leo didn't seem to have any issue talking to Natalie, the commoner, and Natalie would much rather get to know him as herself.

She only hoped she had a chance to see Luca's face when she proved she could surprise him, after all. She had been wrong-footed with him since the start, and she looked forward to finally turning the tables.

# CHAPTER 5

$\mathcal{N}$atalie's temper had abated somewhat by the time she let herself into her room, and she was willing to admit the night hadn't all been terrible. The food had been delicious, and Luca had been an entertaining companion while they ate.

She stretched and shook her head, eager to be free of the constraints of her dress and into a more comfortable nightgown. A few humorous stories weren't enough to make up for Luca's subsequent abandonment. The memory of his wink and wave made her clench her teeth as she slipped off her shoes. He had clearly known what she was about to be subjected to!

Hilary hurried toward her, obviously having drawn the straw for night duty. The other two maids already slept peacefully in cots inside the special alcove designed for their use, but Hilary had been sitting bolt upright in a chair by one window.

From the look of her sleepy eyes, she had been struggling to stay awake, and she didn't ask about the evening as she undid the back of Natalie's dress. As soon as the maid's fumbling, sleep-slowed fingers finished their task, Natalie sent her off to the third cot. Natalie could manage the rest on her own.

The maid went without protest, and Natalie found herself as close to alone as she could hope for while she remained as Rose. Which was yet another reason to swap back immediately. Natalie didn't like the sensation of being hemmed in by nursemaids.

Hilary had left one candelabra still alight, and its glow illuminated Natalie's reflection in the mirror. She sighed as she looked at herself. She had gone to the event with such high hopes. But so far being a princess had not lived up to her expectations.

She was too tired to think about what that meant, and it didn't matter anyway. She was going to set everything right in the morning.

She hurried into her nightgown, but as she slipped into the large bed, she discovered a small slip of folded paper on the pillow. An unfamiliar seal held it closed, giving it an official air, but she couldn't imagine why an official missive would have been left on her bed.

Tugging it open, she held it closer to the candles, her curiosity rising and beginning to drive away the sleepiness. There was no name on the outside, and she opened it on instinct, scanning the contents before she realized her mistake. The note must have been intended for the real Princess Rose.

The words on the page brought her instantly to full wakefulness, and she scanned them a second time, analyzing them more closely. Reading it the first time had been an accident, but now that she had read it, she couldn't pretend not to have done so.

The note clearly contained a threat, although the nature of the threat was vague enough that Natalie wasn't sure what the writer referred to, beyond some link to confidential documents. Clearly the writer expected Rose to understand his references, and he had included the details of a time and place for a secret meeting.

Or the writer could be a she. Natalie knew she shouldn't make assumptions. But both the handwriting and the words gave her a masculine impression, and she couldn't help thinking of the writer as a man. Her eyes kept returning to trace the letters that spelled out *in your best interests*. Clearly some harm was being threatened toward Arcadia, but was the princess in personal danger as well?

Natalie reviewed her short acquaintance with Rose. Something in Rose's manner had changed between Natalie's encounters with her in the Arcadian palace and their journey to Lanover. Rose had claimed it was dissatisfaction with the proposed marriage alliance, but what if it was more than that? Did Rose know she was in danger? Was that why she had suggested they swap places?

But Natalie couldn't believe her new friend would be callously using Natalie as a shield. She tapped the letter against her hand, her thoughts racing. Rose had mentioned the possibility of Natalie receiving notes intended for Rose. And she had stressed that Natalie must send them on to their intended recipient. Rose must plan to go to the meeting, taking the danger on her own shoulders.

Unless she had someone to shelter behind. But Rose's parents had placed their trust in the Lanoverian guards, so no Arcadian guards had accompanied the princess to Lanover. Would she turn to Prince Leo for help, then?

Natalie read the letter again. The writer seemed certain Rose wouldn't involve another kingdom in whatever was going on. His words oozed with the confidence that he faced a nineteen-year-old girl who stood on her own.

But Rose wasn't alone. She had Natalie.

Natalie blew out the candles and lay down, her mind leaping with excitement. With Natalie masquerading in Rose's stead, they had an excellent opportunity to fool the over-confident blackmailer. Surely there was some way to turn the situation to their advantage. Working together with Natalie as Rose and Rose in the background, they could...

Natalie's thoughts came to a halt, a heavy feeling settling over her. Rose hadn't told Natalie of the threat and asked for her help. She had merely instructed her to hand over any notes without reading them. And in the carriage, Rose had defended Natalie's parents, saying that they had acted to protect her. It was a tune Natalie knew all too well.

Natalie's plans for her future were only beginning, which meant she was still just a commoner girl, trying to push her way into the business of royalty. And Natalie had plenty of experience with the response she was likely to receive to that attempt. If she admitted to Rose that she knew about the situation with these confidential documents, Rose would be the one insisting they swap back immediately—and Natalie would find herself shut out of whatever happened next.

By acting alone, Rose would be endangering herself, but

she would consider it a noble sacrifice. And no one would stop to ask Natalie what she thought about the matter—they never did. Neither her abilities nor her desires would factor into the matter at all.

Years of resentment boiled inside her, and she placed the letter under her pillow with a new sense of determination. If one girl was going to take on the risk alone, why should it be Rose?

Natalie had found an opportunity to once again be involved in something that mattered—something that could help people—and she wasn't going to let the chance slip through her fingers. She would find out the blackmailer's intentions without risking Arcadia's only princess. And in the process, she would prove to them all—including Prince Leo—that she was the kind of person who could do what needed to be done.

When she finally slept, her dreams were fitful and troubled, and when she woke, she didn't feel rested. Her determination had not abated, however. She hid the note from the eyes of the three maids and let them dress her in a gown of their choosing, only urging them to hurry. After her late night, she had overslept and was anxious to find Rose.

After accosting five servants in the corridors, Natalie finally found one who could direct her to Rose's hallway, where she was relieved to spot the fourth Arcadian maid, Joanne, emerging from one of the rooms. Joanne looked surprised to see Natalie, but she didn't try to stop her brushing past her and bursting in on the princess.

Natalie stopped just inside the room, her mission momentarily forgotten. Her nose wrinkled as she looked around the small space. It was impossible not to notice the difference between her assigned room and the one she was currently inhabiting.

"Sorry about the room," she said, but Rose waved the apology away with a smile.

"Is everything all right?" the princess asked.

"Yes, I just…wanted to check on you," Natalie said, realizing she should have prepared a more convincing speech in advance.

The note was burning a hole in her pocket, but she couldn't risk blurting out its existence. She needed a subtle way to question the princess and work out what she knew. But subtlety had never been one of Natalie's strengths.

She opened her mouth only to close it again while Rose watched her with a raised brow. Finally the princess broke the silence.

"I hope your room is to your satisfaction," she said.

"Oh yes, it's stunning!" Natalie gushed. "The view is incredible…" Her voice died away as she looked around Rose's room again.

Rose just smiled in amusement. "I'll look forward to seeing it when we switch back places."

Natalie's eyes flew to hers. Only the previous night Natalie had intended to insist they end the ruse, but now she was desperate to last another week until the assigned meeting time. Was Rose about to suggest they switch back immediately? What could Natalie say to delay it if she did?

And why was the meeting date so far away? Did the writer of the note want to leave the princess stressing, just as Natalie was currently doing? Was it all part of some stratagem to—?

Rose spoke, cutting through Natalie's spiraling thoughts.

"You've remembered what I said about not getting into any political discussions, right?" she asked. "And about passing on any letters or notes you receive for me?"

Natalie's mind came into crystal focus. Had she only imagined the extra emphasis Rose had put on the second sentence, and the way the other girl's eyes now bored into her own?

She tried to keep her expression steady as she slowly nodded.

"Yes, of course," she said. "I remember."

She did remember, and now she had further confirmation. Rose was definitely expecting a note of some kind, even if she didn't know its exact contents. And she just as clearly meant to cut Natalie out of whatever was going on.

"I can promise it was nothing but inanities last night," she said with a decent approximation of her usual tone. She allowed a note of dissatisfaction to creep in. "All except one conversation which went on forever and was just a constant stream of reminiscences about your parents and grandparents."

Rose looked alarmed, so Natalie rushed to reassure her.

"Don't worry. I just smiled a lot and said almost nothing, so I don't think I gave anything away."

Rose relaxed. Apparently she wasn't going to insist on an immediate return to their true positions. That was one relief at any rate. Because Natalie was more determined than ever to remain in the princess's role until the nominated time for the secret meeting.

"Please have a seat, Princess Rose." The young noblewoman gestured toward a rich blanket spread out on the grassy hillside.

Cushions had been scattered invitingly across it, and spread out before it was a view of not just the city but also the palace. Clearly the blanket had been placed in the best available spot—but it was also empty.

Natalie forced a smile and sat down, trying to arrange her legs in a graceful manner—a frustratingly difficult feat. When she had accomplished it to the best of her ability, she took a surreptitious look at the other blankets strewn over the grass around her. Each of them contained a group of young people whose conversation and laughter floated across the gentle breeze.

She looked up hopefully at Lady Trina—the host of the event—but the other girl didn't sit.

"I'll have the servants select a plate of delicacies for you to eat." Trina hurried away, intent on her self-assigned task.

Natalie sighed and looked around again. Most of the group had gathered in front of the palace for the walk to the hillside, but Leo had failed to join them. Natalie had assumed that meant he would meet them at their destination. There was still no sign of him, however.

The courtiers in attendance were all young, and Natalie thought she'd met them all the night before. At least, she assumed so, given no one had supplied their names.

If only everyone didn't say the exact same things. Then she might have a hope of remembering everyone's identities.

Trina returned, and Natalie smiled as welcomingly as she could. But as soon as Trina had delivered the plate of food, someone called to her, and she bustled off, visibly full of the importance of hosting.

Natalie sighed again.

"You don't need to glare at the food so ferociously," said a laughing voice. "I promise I didn't prepare this menu either."

Natalie looked up. "Oh. It's you." She wanted company, just not this company.

Luca's lips twitched. "I'm sorry to disappoint." He threw himself down beside her, lounging comfortably among the cushions.

Natalie looked behind him hopefully. If Luca had just arrived on the hillside, maybe his cousin had too. There was no sign of Prince Leo, however.

She deflated, fiddling with the closest cushion and trying not to sigh yet again. From the corner of her eye, she caught Luca watching her, curiosity gleaming in his eyes.

He must think her very unlike a proper princess. She sat up straight and pasted on her best royal smile.

"Your Highness!" Trina returned, slightly out of breath, as if she'd hurried straight back from whatever hosting responsibilities had occupied her. "I'm so sorry for the interruption. There are certain complications with this location, but I was sure you would appreciate the view of our beautiful city and consider it worth any inconveniences."

"Lanare is stunning," Natalie said with sincerity.

The southern kingdom was entrancing—utterly unlike her own home in the mountains. But she couldn't add that, so she fell silent.

Trina bobbed a shallow curtsy to Luca. "I'm so glad you could make it, Prince Luca. I was sorry to hear Prince Leo had other duties that required his attention."

Luca smiled, his manner easy. "It's Leo's loss. He would much prefer to be outside than stuck behind a desk." His expression suggested Leo was well known for this trait, and Trina laughed. Natalie chuckled as well, a beat behind. "But with his parents away, he takes his responsibilities seriously," Luca added.

"Of course!" Trina said quickly. "You must let him know that we all completely understand. It's our honor to help entertain Princess Rose during her visit."

She beamed at Natalie but took the first opportunity to hurry away. She seemed to consider herself relieved from the duty of entertaining her guest of honor now that Luca had appeared to keep Natalie company.

Natalie watched her go disconsolately. "So honored she

needed to run for the other side of the hilltop," she muttered.

Luca laughed, and Natalie flushed. She'd spoken without thinking. Rose would never say something so impolite about her host.

"I'm sorry to hear you don't feel honored," Luca said with a wicked twinkle. "When you've been given the very best rug—and so much space!"

Natalie glared at him. "Yes. It's a reminder of all the *space* you gave me last night."

Luca tried to look contrite and failed utterly. She suspected he didn't know how.

"It's best to remove the bandage all at once," he told her solemnly. "Now you've spoken to every one of the elderly courtiers left in the capital, and you can safely avoid them for the rest of your visit."

"Can I just as safely avoid you?" she asked sweetly, and he grinned.

"Ah, but I'm much more nimble than the average eighty-year-old. And people do keep inviting me to everything."

Natalie looked back over the assembled young people. "Leo was invited, too, but he didn't feel the need to show up."

"Yes, but that's because he has *responsibilities*," Luca said.

Natalie cast him a suspicious glance. Something in his tone hinted at unspoken meaning behind his words. Did Luca see her as a responsibility?

She looked around a little more wildly, hoping to see another familiar face—any other familiar face—walking past. Where was Rose? She'd been at the reception the previous evening. Surely she didn't intend to abandon Natalie to handle all the remaining events alone.

"Are you used to something different in the Arcadian court?" Luca asked, something in his tone making the question sound more earnest than his earlier quips.

Natalie thought back to the few days she had spent at the Arcadian capital. She had certainly never seen Rose standing alone at any social occasion. But Rose would disapprove of her speaking rudely to one of Lanover's royal princes, and Natalie had already forgotten herself several times.

"I suppose it's different there," she said cautiously. "Since everyone knows me. They're not so…careful."

Luca's lips twitched, and he glanced toward Trina. "Lady Trina does seem unusually *careful.*" He grinned at her. "What an excellent word, by the way. It's not normally what she's known for either. I wonder what has her on edge." He watched Trina across the hilltop before smiling at what seemed to be a private joke. "Of course Leo isn't the only one flexing his muscles while his parents are away. Trina's parents probably gave her a lecture before they left about not embarrassing the family in front of visiting royalty."

If that was the explanation for Trina's behavior, then all the other young nobles must have received similar lectures. Either that, or they were wary of her potential to upend their hierarchy. Perhaps it was both.

She wished she could announce to them all that she—or rather Rose—had no intention of marrying their crown prince. And neither were they going to offend Arcadia and disgrace their families over a misspoken word.

"But don't worry," Luca said, his eyes laughing at her depressed expression. "There's only about twenty more families left to have their turn playing host."

"Twenty?" Natalie stared at him. "Do you mean we'll be doing this for the entire visit?"

He glanced at the view. "I imagine some of the events will be indoors."

Natalie glared at him, trying to ignore the headache forming behind her temples. She felt exhausted, although the walk to the picnic had been done at a gentle pace and she had already been sitting for some time. She had never enjoyed small talk, but she had never realized how utterly draining it could be either.

Luca shifted closer to her, his voice dropping low. "Not every Lanoverian has been lectured on being careful."

Natalie remained ramrod straight, refusing to mirror his motions and lean toward him. She gave him a reproving look.

"If you tell me your parents have never lectured you about being careful, I'll call you a liar."

He laughed, unabashed. "The word might have been thrown around once or twice, but never in connection with your name, I assure you."

Natalie raised her brows. She would have liked to know what he *had* been told regarding Princess Rose, but she refused to give him the satisfaction of asking.

"Social events don't have to be dull," Luca said with an expressive look. "We can always entertain each other by being...reckless."

Natalie jumped to her feet, shaking out her skirts. "Last night, you abandoned me to an entire gaggle of octogenarians and ran for it. Without shame, I might add. And now you want me to entertain myself by flirting with you?"

Luca stood slowly, easy elegance in all his movements. He adopted an expression of hurt. "I don't remember saying anything about flirting. I would never offend a foreign princess with such a suggestion."

Natalie's eyes narrowed, and she turned to march toward the other side of the hill—a move that would have been more effective if Luca didn't easily match her stride, grinning down at her as he kept pace. The man was both infuriating and impossible to shake.

"Do you really mean to shadow me everywhere I go?" she asked icily.

"Not at all," Luca said promptly. "Say the word, and I'll leave you to stand in state alone on the top of the hill."

Natalie glanced at the occupants of the other picnic rugs—none of whom showed any inclination to leave their settled positions.

"Fine," she said with what grace she could muster. "If you must follow me, you can occupy yourself by telling me about the city." She pointed toward the buildings below them and the various landmarks that were visible from a distance.

Luca grinned and launched into guide mode, his tales about his city proving both informative and interesting. Natalie might even have forgiven him for being the wrong prince and allowed herself to feel grateful for his presence, except that she kept catching him laughing at her with his eyes. He seemed determined to infuriate her, though she had no idea why he was treating the supposed Arcadian princess in such a fashion. He certainly made it impossible to adopt a proper princess manner back to him.

Whatever his reasons, she was relieved to lose him in the throng of courtiers descending the hill at the end of the event, and she resolved to avoid him as much as possible in future.

Her resolution proved difficult to keep, however. As Luca had predicted, a seemingly endless number of the younger members of court took turns hosting events for their peers and the visiting princess. And as Natalie had feared, the young courtiers continued to hold her at arms' length, their conversation painfully polite and shallow.

To make matters worse, Leo was rarely present, and she concluded that he could only be guaranteed to turn up to events he was personally hosting. Even Rose failed to appear more often than not. Only Luca reliably attended each event, his words—whether teasing or serious—always accompanied by the laugh in his eyes that told her he viewed her as a game.

Natalie would have happily relinquished Rose's identity several times over if it wasn't for the intrigue of the note and her concern over the upcoming meeting. It was the only thing that drove her through each exhausting day.

# CHAPTER 7

When the end of the first week brought a ride along the coast—this time hosted by Prince Leo—Natalie donned her riding habit with relief. She would finally have the chance to have a proper conversation with the elusive crown prince.

Her good spirits rose even further when the riders gathered in front of the palace, and she found no sign of Luca in their midst. Rose had already promised to help Natalie position herself beside Leo during the ride, and if Luca was absent for once, then her path was clear.

The groomsman leading the ride called for the riders to gather up. Natalie released a pleased sigh and directed her mount forward. But a flicker of movement to one side caught her eye, and she looked around in time to see a final, belated rider appearing from the direction of the stables.

Luca.

Her hands tightened on her reins, causing her mare to

whinny and dance in place. She forced her grip to relax, but her eyes lingered on the straight form of the prince.

The problem, she told herself with a savage mental voice, was that he looked far better on horseback than anyone had the right to look. And when he caught her gaze across the crowd—and *winked*—her pulse took off in defiance of her furious mind.

She looked away. She refused to find anyone so thoroughly bothersome to be pulse-racingly attractive. Her heart rate needed to get itself under control. There was no reason for such foolishness. The two royal cousins looked strikingly similar, and yet the sight of Leo on his horse hadn't sent her heart into foolish spasms.

She forced her eyes to stay fixed on Leo, taking note of his excellent seat and his firm hands on his horse's reins. He clearly knew how to ride every bit as well as Luca—No! She would not allow her thoughts to circle back to that tiresome man. She finally had the chance to make a favorable impression on the crown prince, and she refused to let Luca get under her skin. The man was clearly doing it on purpose—and finding it amusing!

Despite the grooms and guards clearing a path for them, the riders had to thread their way through the city in single file, passing the docks and heading north beyond the edge of the city. There, the coastal road allowed room for two to comfortably ride side-by-side, and everyone regrouped. The ride was intended for pleasure, so the groom at the front set a comfortable pace that allowed the riders to converse easily and admire the view of the sea.

As promised, Rose maneuvered her horse neatly, ensuring Natalie and Leo ended up riding together.

The crown prince smiled at her. "How have you been enjoying the whirlwind of court events? I did try to convince my people that you don't need to be occupied every waking moment, but they seem determined to outdo each other."

"I would have enjoyed the events more if you were there." She gave him her most endearing smile.

He looked regretful, but she suspected the emotion was only skin deep. If he'd really wanted to be there, surely he could have found a way.

"I gave my cousin strict instructions to make sure you were well entertained." He glanced behind them to where Luca was riding with Rose. "I hope he hasn't been shirking his duty."

Natalie tried to think of something diplomatic to say and failed.

"Not that it was a burdensome order," Leo said quickly, seeming to realize his possible misstep. "I believe he's been enjoying himself greatly."

Natalie ground her teeth together. One of them had been having a marvelous time, certainly.

Silence fell between them.

The road sloped down until it was separated from the sand by only a thin stretch of grass. Earlier, the beach had been rocky, but a long, sandy stretch now beckoned, the white sand contrasting with the brilliant blue of the ocean.

Luca took advantage of the strip of grass to appear on Leo's other side, his eyes glinting in the bright sunshine and his dark hair lightened to burnished chestnut.

"Race along the beach, Leo?" he challenged.

His cousin gave him a repressive look, his eyes flicking subtly toward Natalie.

Luca just laughed. "Don't let Lila hold you back. I'm sure she thinks she can beat us both." He leaned forward to give Natalie the same challenging look he'd just given Leo.

"Of course I could," she replied, nettled. Her parents had tried to make up for barring her from court by buying her a horse, and Natalie had rarely lost a race on her prized mare.

"Then prove it! Race you to that spot where the rock juts out of the water!" Luca urged his horse down toward the sand with a carefree whoop.

"Cheater!" Natalie cried, outraged. Typical that he would try to steal an early start.

Forgetting all about her earlier resolution, she galloped her mare onto the sand after Luca. From the moment she had met the infuriating prince, he had been playing a game with her—a game with rules she didn't understand. Hampered by her false identity, Natalie's hands had been tied, and she'd suffered loss after loss. But for once, she was going to triumph over the smugly confident Prince Luca.

Her whole focus narrowed to the rider in front of her and the pounding of her horse's hooves against the sand. The mare was smaller than Luca's mount, but Natalie had sensed the fire in her belly as soon as she'd swung onto the horse's back. They had chosen one of their best mounts for the visiting princess.

She urged the horse faster, whispering encouragements as they slowly gained ground on the larger, heavier rider ahead of them. When she finally pulled even, and her mare, scenting the victory, surged forward, Natalie looked back and gave a whoop of her own.

The patch of rock flashed past them, and Luca pulled up, slowing his horse gradually as he shook his head in defeat. Natalie slowed also, allowing him to catch up and ride beside her. For once his eyes held a look that she interpreted as begrudging respect, and she intended to savor every moment.

Her hair had come loose in the wind of the ride, and she ran her hands through it, shaking it free. Tipping her head back, she closed her eyes to enjoy the feel of the sun on her face. The salt air and the sound of the waves made her feel freer than she had done since arriving in Lanover.

"This is the way to live, isn't it?" Luca asked, and for once, Natalie couldn't disagree with his sentiment.

She nodded her agreement, opening her eyes to find him watching her with an unfamiliar look in his eyes that made her clear her throat and look around for the others. The double line of riders had followed them down onto the sand, but their sedate pace meant they were still some way behind.

Leo and Rose had pulled ahead of the others, however, and were approaching more quickly.

Luca and Natalie turned back to join them, and Natalie greeted them with a smile, her mood still high after the exhilarating ride. But Rose pulled away from Leo, directing her own mare close to Natalie's and hissing at her under her breath.

"Quick, put your hair back up before the others reach us and get a proper look at you! What were you thinking?! Princesses are supposed to behave with more decorum!"

Her eyes conveyed the rest of her message. Natalie wasn't out for a ride with a friend but as part of an official event with the Lanoverian court. And the courtiers weren't seeing Natalie behaving like a hoyden but the Arcadian princess behaving that way.

Her joy instantly drained away.

"I've lost most of my pins!" she whispered back, frantic. "I'll never be able to get my hair respectable again."

Rose hesitated, clearly unsure what to suggest.

Leo cleared his throat, urging his horse closer to them. "If you'd like to return to the palace, Lila, I can escort you there myself."

Natalie looked at him gratefully, but Luca spoke before she could reply.

"Don't forget you're the host today, Leo. You can't leave. But I can escort Lila back if she wishes to go."

Natalie's heart sank, but she could hardly demand that the crown prince leave his own event to accompany her, especially when she had been the one to cause a problem in the first place. She shouldn't have shaken free her pins. If she still had them, she and Rose might have been able to achieve something vaguely respectable.

Cowed by her own thoughtlessness, she accepted Luca's unwelcome escort in silence. And despite his cajoling attempts to coax her into speech, she remained silent the whole way back to the palace.

The day had turned out nothing like she'd planned. She'd barely exchanged a few stilted sentences with Leo before she'd so far forgotten herself as to embarrass Rose and humiliate herself in the process.

It had all been Luca's fault! If only he hadn't challenged

her to race. Natalie had never been good at refusing such challenges—she had too much fondness for winning.

When they reached the palace gardens, Luca finally dropped his teasing tone and spoke in a serious voice that caught her attention, his words earnest.

"I'm sorry, Lila. I didn't mean to ruin your afternoon. I got caught up in my love of racing and didn't think it through."

What could Natalie say to that? It was almost exactly what she had just been reproaching herself for. But she was too bitterly disappointed to entirely let go of her anger.

"If you're sorry," she snapped, the words coming out harshly, "you'll stop hounding me everywhere I go!"

She swung down from her horse, handing the reins to the closest groom. Not waiting for Luca's reply, she hurried into the palace.

She knew she'd been unreasonably harsh, but she kept fleeing anyway—knowing deep down that she was actually fleeing from the unsettling look she had seen in his eyes twice that day.

When she reached her room, she collapsed onto her bed and cried herself out, cursing yet another useless restriction on the life of a princess. The goal she had been chasing for years was looking less and less shiny every day.

She still longed to be involved in important matters like unmasking the villain blackmailing and threatening Rose. But how much pain, exhaustion, and daily boredom was she willing to endure in order to secure that future? Natalie had thought she knew the answer, but she was no longer so sure.

# CHAPTER 8

Natalie lay awake half the night wondering what the next day would bring. After her mistake on the beach, there was every chance Rose would demand they swap back immediately. After all, they had never intended their ruse to last longer than a week. But the appointed meeting time was only the next night, and Natalie couldn't afford to shock the entire court until after she'd unmasked the blackmailer.

If word reached him about the girls' ruse, there was every chance he wouldn't show up. Prince Leo might even kick Natalie out of Lanare, making it impossible for her to appear at the designated gazebo where the meeting was supposed to occur. She certainly hadn't succeeded in forging a strong enough emotional bond with the crown prince that he would forgive her the deception.

But she made it through breakfast without hearing the dreaded knock on her door, and she began to hope again. Unable to bear the idea of incessant, meaningless small talk, Natalie excused herself from the day's activities and shut herself in her room. She would have opened it for Rose, of course, but when Luca came to the door and tried to cajole her out, she refused to speak to him. Eventually, Cate sent him away.

Eventually even the three maids fled the room, sick of Natalie's constant pacing and refusal to answer any questions. They had probably gone to Rose to complain, but Natalie was past caring. Surely she had made it far enough through the day that Rose wouldn't insist on exposing their ruse that evening.

Darkness finally arrived, and Natalie ate the evening meal from a tray in her room. The maids still hadn't returned, so she didn't have to pretend to go to bed as the interminable minutes ticked slowly by, counting down the hours until the meeting time.

Eventually she decided the hour had advanced enough that she could justify leaving the palace. She wanted to be in place—hiding somewhere near the gazebo where she could observe without being seen—well before the allotted time. But she had a realistic understanding of how long she would be able to maintain a position of silent watchfulness. It wouldn't do to be there too early.

Finding a place to hide proved more difficult than she had anticipated, however. There were plenty of positions that allowed her to remain completely out of sight, but they left her own view of the gazebo entirely obscured. By the opposite token, she could find plenty of vantage points that gave her a good view, but anyone in the gazebo would be able to see her just as easily.

She had chosen her darkest, simplest dress to wear, but even so, she wasn't exactly inconspicuous. She tried one spot and then another, always conscious of the time. It had passed painfully slowly all day only to now accelerate to terrifying speeds.

Eventually she accepted that a perfect spot couldn't be found and settled herself behind a bush that was large enough to obscure her while still allowing at least a limited viewpoint through the spring growth of leaves.

And then she waited. Time slowed back down to a crawl. Her crouching position wasn't as stable as she would have liked, and when a bug flew past her ear, her instinctive attempt to swat it away nearly unbalanced her completely. But if she sat, it would be too hard to move quickly, and if she stood, she would be visible behind the foliage.

She resettled with a fresh edge of tension. She couldn't afford to do anything like that once her target arrived. Her position wasn't hidden enough that she would go unnoticed if she started thrashing around.

Finally she heard footsteps approaching, soft and hurried on a gravel path. She froze, peering through the leaves with desperate intensity. She had been waiting a week for this moment, and she couldn't fail in her task of identifying the man threatening Rose.

A masculine figure came into view, glancing back over his shoulder as he walked. She waited, not even breathing, until he turned back to face her. But the sight of his face gave her no clue to his identity. He had swathed himself in black from head to toe, and there was nothing distinctive about his silhouette.

The man twitched, jumping as the breeze rustled the leaves around him. He hurried the last few steps into the gazebo, only to halt abruptly when he realized it was empty. A softly spoken curse reached her ears.

Natalie considered her options. He had come alone as she had hoped, which allowed the possibility of jumping out and accosting him. But he was taller than she was and moved with an ease that suggested he was still young. If he ran, she might not catch him, and if she did catch him, it might not go well for her.

Either way, he wasn't likely to answer any demands for information.

She could approach more sedately in her guise as Rose and claim to have been running late. But she still didn't know if her adversary intended physical harm to Rose, nor did she know if he was aware of the true appearance of the princess.

She could claim to be one of Rose's maids, sent in her place, but she should have worn a different dress if she wanted to pull off that lie. And he looked jumpy enough that he might run even if he believed her claim.

There was only one real option. She had to wait and follow him when he left. She wasn't able to see his face, but she still had a chance to find out his identity.

The minutes drew out as the waiting man became visibly impatient. When he began cursing more loudly and looking toward the rising moon, Natalie let out a long, silent breath. He was surely close to leaving.

She adjusted her position, moving her weight quietly, poised to leap up when required. Any moment now, the man was going to give up on Rose and leave.

"Lila? What are you doing there?" The piercing whisper

startled Natalie so badly she lost her balance entirely, barely stifling a scream.

Her target froze for less than a second before taking off down the nearest path at a sprint. Natalie struggled to her feet and took a step after him. But he had already disappeared out of sight in the dark garden. Forewarned and with a head start, he would be impossible to follow.

She spun on the new arrival, furious.

"Lila?" Luca asked again, peering past her shoulder. "Was there someone else there? That sounded like footsteps."

He hadn't even seen the man in the gazebo! He had just wandered through this particular part of the gardens at the worst possible moment. Of course he would show up and ruin all her plans!

"What is wrong with you?" Her chest heaved, her eyes flashing her anger. "Why do you always have to push in where you're not wanted?"

"What are you talking about?" He lightly grasped her arm. "Lila, what are you doing out here in the middle of the night? No one's seen you all day."

"Am I not allowed one day to myself?" Natalie trembled in the wake of both the earlier tension and the crushing disappointment. "Is that the cost of being a princess? I can't have a moment to myself?"

Luca frowned, peering at her face in the partial light of the moon. "You're serious." He let her go and took a step back. "You're truly upset."

"I'm always upset with you," she snapped back, but he shook his head.

"No, this is different. In the past—that was a game, of sorts. But tonight, you're truly angry. What did I do?"

He looked over her shoulder again, his face tightening. "Were you meeting someone?"

"No!" she snapped. "I wasn't. Not that it's any business of yours."

"Then why are you out here?" he repeated. "And why are you so angry?"

Natalie drew in a shaking breath. "Never mind. It's too late now anyway. Just for once, *leave me be*."

She stalked toward the palace, expecting to hear his footsteps on the gravel behind her. But apparently he had respected her words. For once he made no further move to push himself into her orbit.

# CHAPTER 9

Natalie visited the gazebo as soon as it was light the next morning, searching for clues. But she wasn't surprised when she turned up nothing. Collapsing onto one of the structure's bench seats, she sighed.

After all her waiting, she had nothing.

She straightened. Not entirely nothing. Rose hadn't turned up, which confirmed she hadn't known about the meeting. The note Natalie still held had been the only communication about it.

Had the time come to talk to the princess about the situation? Show her the note? Natalie had delayed doing so until she could uncover the identity of the blackmailer and turn the tables against him. But she'd failed abysmally at that.

She considered her options. Her failure at the potential meeting had only increased the likelihood that Rose would respond to her revelation by insisting they switch back and then shutting Natalie out entirely. Her blackmailer was probably insisting on her silence, so if she was scared enough—for both Natalie and herself—she might even send Natalie away from Lanover altogether. But in so doing, she would create all sorts of rumors—ones that might alert the blackmailer to their ruse. If he guessed someone else had been involved, who knew what retaliation he would take on Rose.

Natalie had to remain in her current role. They couldn't afford to have the whole court talking about them and their deception. Not yet anyway.

She hurried down the gazebo steps, lost in her thoughts as she strode through the gardens. If she couldn't go to Rose, could she tell someone else?

An image of Luca flashed into her mind, but she shook it away with an impatient gesture. He'd caused nothing but trouble so far.

The crown prince was an option, though. He might have the capacity to protect both Rose and Natalie. But what would he make of the note? Would he suspect Rose of being complicit? Or blame her for bringing Arcadia's problems into Lanover?

The princess had stressed the importance of not allowing their charade to cause an international incident. And this was something far more serious than a brief, mischievous swapping of identities. If Natalie ran to Prince Leo, she might create exactly the sort of incident they needed to avoid.

As she reached a side door of the palace, she sighed. If matters got too out of hand, she would have no choice but to go to Leo. But there had been no direct threat of violence so far, so she could risk waiting a little longer. As long as she was still Rose, another possibility might present itself to her.

As she slipped back into her luxurious chamber, she admitted to herself that the room no longer brought her any joy. She was heartily sick of the role she had adopted. She didn't regret the blackmailer's note accidentally falling into her hands, but all the other parts of playing a princess had been oppressive and burdensome. The role hadn't even allowed her to get close to Leo. Her goal of winning the crown prince was as far removed as ever, and Natalie couldn't even bring herself to care. It was becoming increasingly difficult to remember why she had been so convinced that becoming a queen would solve her problems.

Natalie rejoined the activities of court with even less enthusiasm than previously. Instead of getting easier, the necessary smiles and pleasantries required an increasingly difficult effort.

At least the food remained excellent, and she was finally being left in peace. After her outburst in the garden, Luca was keeping his distance.

*It was a relief*, she told herself firmly. The absence of the prince and his verbal sparring had nothing whatsoever to do with why the social events felt extra flat. She even managed to muster some enthusiasm when an afternoon picnic in the garden turned out to be enlivened with a friendly archery competition.

The armsmaster had set up a number of targets on a

patch of grass, and the guests took turns showing off their skill. Those not participating occupied themselves with the picnic food or cheered for their friends' efforts.

Natalie stood watching the archers with avid interest and a touch of wistfulness. She would have preferred to be a participant than a spectator.

"Should I assume you shoot as well as you ride, Lila?" a familiar voice asked.

She turned slowly to find Luca at her side, wearing his old grin. Her heart most definitely did not make any sort of happy leap at the sight. She was just starved for conversation that wasn't completely inane.

"Actually, I've never shot before," she admitted. "My mother said that I was quite dangerous enough without a bow in my hands, and that if I was determined to learn, I could wait until I was eighteen."

Luca gave a surprised laugh, and Natalie belatedly remembered she was supposed to be the princess of Arcadia. She bit her lip, but Luca didn't question her slip.

"In that case, you'll have to allow me to teach you."

She caught a note of hesitancy from him, his eyes offering a subtle challenge, as if he thought she needed goading in order to accept his offer. He was vastly underestimating her desire to learn archery, however.

"Can we start right now?" She barely refrained from bouncing on the balls of her feet.

He laughed. "I don't see why not. I'm fairly confident in my ability to prevent you shooting another guest by accident."

She laughed herself. "Then you'll have my appreciation. I'm reasonably sure that shooting a member of the

Lanoverian court would cause the sort of international incident I've been instructed to avoid."

"You're full of surprises, Lila," he murmured softly, and Natalie tensed.

But he turned away immediately to procure her a bow and quiver of arrows, freeing her from the necessity of responding. Even so, her exuberant excitement dulled, replaced by wariness. What had he meant by that comment?

Had he been looking into her in the days since their encounter in the garden? Was that why he'd been absent? What had he found?

"Relax, Lila! You're far too tense," he said as she tried to follow his instructions and fit her first arrow to the bow.

She barely refrained from rolling her eyes. Who exactly was the source of all her tension?

But she had no desire for him to know how nervous his curiosity made her. She rolled her shoulders and let out a slow breath before trying again.

"Better!" he said approvingly, and she managed a natural smile.

But when she released the arrow, it didn't fly straight into the center of the target as she had envisioned. Instead it plopped into the grass disappointingly short of its aim. She pursed her lips, and he laughed.

"If you hit the target on your first attempt, you'd be a prodigy."

"I would have liked to be a shooting prodigy," she said wistfully, and he shook his head, his eyes dancing.

"It might be better for all of us that you're not. Think of your poor mother's nerves."

She laughed, her tension easing even more.

"You need to pull the string back further." He took it from her and demonstrated. "And hold it steadier."

He talked her through her second attempt, giving her enough tips that she managed to propel the arrow the needed distance. Unfortunately her aim suffered as a result, and it came nowhere near hitting the target.

"Bad luck," Luca said with a straight face. "There was a puff of wind."

Natalie gave him an irritated look. "My pride isn't that fragile."

He came close beside her. "You need to aim—" He hesitated. "Do you mind if I...?" He gestured to indicate he wanted to move her physically into the right position.

She nodded, her attention on the target, so the feel of his chest against her back and his arms encircling hers took her by surprise. She bit short her soft gasp. She should have realized what he meant, and she wasn't going to give him the satisfaction of knowing he had affected her.

She kept her eyes on the target. But while she could pretend to be focused only on the archery, she couldn't actually ignore the warmth of his body or the strength in his arms as he guided her into the right position.

"That's it," he murmured in her ear, and his breath on her skin sent goosebumps racing down her neck.

She swallowed, and he drew back slightly, letting her go. With an effort of will—and a reminder that it was only Luca beside her, not someone worthy of shivers or goosebumps despite his distracting looks—she steadied herself. The arrow flew from her bow and bumped against one side of the target, falling to the grass.

"I did it!" She turned her head to look at him and froze.

He had only moved half a step away and was looking down at her, their faces now only inches apart. She took in the golden flecks in the brown of his eyes and wondered where all the air had gone.

"A very interesting mystery," he breathed, the words so quiet she wasn't sure if he realized he'd spoken aloud.

She immediately stepped back, and he mirrored her movement, clearing his throat as he did so.

"Keep practicing like that, and you'll soon have it," he said. "And while you do, I'll go and fetch you a plate of food. Shooting is hungry work." He strode quickly away.

Natalie watched him put distance between them with a furrow in her brow, her thoughts far from archery. Luca was definitely suspicious of her. She needed to be more careful.

And she needed to find a way to track down Rose's blackmailer and expose him. Then she and Rose could tell everyone the truth, and Luca would have all his answers. He would switch his dutiful—if impudent—attentions to their proper target, and Natalie would never have to be bothered by him again.

The thought brought surprisingly little comfort, but she turned back to the target, determined to stay focused. It didn't matter what happened after they revealed the truth. She just needed to make sure Luca didn't find it out for himself before she was ready to relinquish Rose's place.

She shot at the target again and again, on edge as she waited for him to return. But when she'd emptied the quiver, she turned to find a plate of food perched on a nearby stone balustrade with no sign of Luca.

Her eyes sought him out, and she located him some distance away, talking to two young men of court. Their eyes instantly met, but he didn't leave his conversation or return to her.

He kept his distance for the rest of the afternoon. But even if he didn't speak to her, she felt his eyes burning into her and felt the pressure of his watchful gaze.

Natalie arrived at the evening's reception with nerves stretched thin. All around her, others laughed and called to each other, spirits high after the afternoon's archery, but Natalie couldn't enter into their good humor.

When she spotted Rose coming toward her, she ducked into the closest clump of people and started for the opposite side of the room. She couldn't risk Rose asking her to swap back places. She wasn't ready yet.

She hid behind a potted plant, too on edge even for the refreshment table. But beyond her hiding place, laughter continued to swirl through the room, growing louder until someone called for a dance.

"Yes! Yes!" several voices echoed. "We must dance!"

Either Prince Leo or the staff must have anticipated the request because musicians appeared on cue. Couples began to form, but Natalie didn't move from her hiding place. She knew she was missing her chance to dance with Leo—even with informal dancing, the crown prince was sure to ask the Arcadian princess to open the dancing with him. But she couldn't bring herself to have any interest in a duty dance with Prince Leo.

The dance began, and she soon caught sight of Leo dancing with the highest-ranked Lanoverian girl present. Rose was among the throng as well, on the arm of one of the court men. The only face Natalie didn't see was Luca.

Where was he? Off searching her room for clues?

He wouldn't find anything there. She kept the note tucked on her person at all times so the maids wouldn't find it, and she and Rose had already swapped any items that might be incriminating.

"Lila!" Luca's voice made her start. "Why are you hiding back here?"

"I'm not hiding," she said, but her words lacked any heat.

"If you're not hiding, then you'll have no objection to dancing." He held out his hand in a movement that was half invitation, half silent command.

The lively notes of the current song wound down, and the instruments paused briefly as they prepared to start another melody. Natalie responded by instinct, placing her hand in his. She had always liked to dance, and hiding had never been her style.

Luca pulled her onto the dance floor just as the second song started. It was the strains of a waltz. His hand encircled her waist, and she sucked in an involuntary breath. But she let him pull her close as the dance demanded, clasping her hand in his.

He spun them into the swirl of dancers, and heat raced

up her spine. Her heart beat an irregular rhythm, making it hard to think.

She had to be careful of Luca. He was suspicious of her.

When she worked up the courage to look up into his eyes, his intense gaze trapped hers. He seemed to be trying to search out all her secrets with his eyes alone. She shivered, and he pulled her even closer, the two of them alone in a sea of dancers.

Natalie wanted to push him away and run from the room. She wanted to pull him even closer still. She wanted to tell him to stop looking at her like that.

She did nothing.

"What secrets are you hiding, Lila?" he murmured in a husky voice.

Her heart beat even faster, her eyes still trapped in his. He had been pushing her since the moment she arrived, teasing her, testing her. But she refused to back down. A different kind of fire licked up her spine.

"My secrets are my own," she said.

Something like disappointment flashed in his eyes, and he broke the magnetic gaze between them. It didn't feel like a victory.

"I know there's something you're not telling me," he said quietly. "I just wish you would trust me. Whatever it is, I can help you."

"Can you?" she whispered under her breath.

He caught the words, pulling her all the way against his chest and trapping her eyes again.

"I'm more capable than you seem to think."

She swallowed, wavering. But it wasn't his capability she questioned, it was his loyalty. He didn't know that she kept more secrets than just her own, or that they involved both Arcadia and Lanover.

Or perhaps he guessed as much. Perhaps it was his loyalty to Lanover that prompted the question as he sought out the thorn that had wedged itself in his court.

His arms, still warm and strong, held her close. But her thoughts no longer wavered. She looked up at him with defiance in her eyes.

"I am capable also, Prince Luca. If I need your help, I will ask for it."

"Will you?" he whispered, half to himself, sparks in his eyes as he held hers.

His face swayed even closer, but the movements of the dance had spun them to the edge of the floor, and she pulled out of his arms. Ignoring the coldness that washed over her at his absence, she stood alone.

"You asked me to trust you. Perhaps you should consider trusting me." Turning on her heels, she left the receiving room, the fire along her spine driving her all the way to her room.

But inside—as Hilary helped her unfasten her dress— she admitted to herself that her usual self-confidence had dimmed. She had always believed that if she wanted something, she merely had to go and fight for it. Now she wondered what good it was to fight when she was no longer sure what she was even fighting for. What use was all her confidence if she could no longer see her way?

She parted the covers only to pause, her whole body going rigid. Another note on her pillow, identical in appearance to the last. She turned to ask Hillary where it had come from, but the other girl had already disappeared to her cot.

Natalie remembered belatedly why she couldn't mention the notes to the maids—their loyalty was to Rose. She angled her body to conceal it from view as she opened it. Her fingers trembled as she read the words inside.

An angry hand had written in bold, slashing letters. The message upbraided her for failing to appear at the designated meeting and threatened to disappear forever.

Natalie read the words a second time. The first note had made it clear he was blackmailing Rose over something, but now it was obvious he had something Rose desperately wanted.

Guilt stirred within her. After her failure to appear at the first meeting, the man could have disappeared forever, taking whatever Rose needed with him.

He hadn't done so, however, instead writing to her again with fresh demands. He didn't intend to risk a face-to-face meeting a second time. Instead he had taken a different sort of risk—putting his demands down on paper.

In exchange for whatever he had stolen from Arcadia, he wanted a selection of private Lanoverian documents and one of their official seals. The writer described a hidden place to leave them and warned Rose not to test him again. Only once the documents were secure would he return what she sought.

Natalie blew out the candle, her whole body quivering somewhere between shock and excitement. What had the man stolen from Arcadia that was so valuable he could use it to blackmail a princess? And what should Natalie do now she knew what he wanted?

Talking to one of the Lanoverian princes was out of the question. If they thought for even a second that Rose intended to betray Lanoverian secrets in exchange for Arcadian ones, they might have her arrested.

Although there would be some complications to deal with if they arrested a foreign princess. They could send her home, though. And they could arrest Natalie with impunity.

Natalie couldn't tell Rose either. She felt sure the Arcadian princess wouldn't want to harm Lanover. But Natalie couldn't be completely sure Rose wouldn't feel cornered into doing so. When it came to the matter of loyalty, Rose's would obviously lie with Arcadia first.

But Natalie had been thinking of Lanover as her future home for three years. Her loyalty lay with the southern kingdom over Arcadia, despite her friendship with Rose. There was no way she would give the blackmailer the items he wanted—nor would she let Rose do so. The documents sounded highly confidential, and the seal was utterly out of the question. He could do enormous harm with a stolen seal.

So, once again, her best option was to remain as Rose and find out everything she could about the blackmailer. As long as Rose didn't know what the blackmailer was demanding, Lanover was safe. And if Natalie could find out enough details about the man, she might be able to help Arcadia as well.

Fresh energy coursed through Natalie now that she once again had a goal and a focus. This was why she had wanted to become a queen in the first place. She might be acting alone, but she would find a way to defeat the man who had the audacity to threaten a princess and cheat a kingdom.

# CHAPTER 11

The next day, Natalie once again shut herself in her room. This time she sent the three maids away at the start of the day, needing uninterrupted peace for her task.

Once alone, however, she sat motionless for an extended period. How did you write an official document?

Her first two attempts were soon abandoned, thrown into the fire to hide any trace of her efforts. But once the words began to flow, she wrote at speed, thinking of the documents she had sometimes found on her parents' desk. She even began to enjoy using pompous-sounding words to string together endless waffle.

The false documents she was creating didn't actually say anything sensible. They just needed to be convincing at a quick glance. Given how twitchy the blackmailer had been at the gazebo, she was betting he wouldn't look at the documents too closely before hurrying out of the palace grounds.

Once she'd followed him back to his base of operations,

it wouldn't matter when he discovered the ruse. She could send the royal guards after him and put an end to the whole business.

Thankfully she didn't have to attempt creating a fake seal—a task that would have been much more difficult than writing false documents. Natalie had one of her own she could use, a parting gift from her younger sister. Rebecca had almost certainly intended it as a jest—she had considered Natalie's quest both ridiculous and doomed to failure —but Natalie had thrown it in the bottom of her bag anyway.

She dug it out, leaving it in its leather pouch. Like the documents, it would only fool a cursory look. But she was trusting that was all the man would stop to give it.

Documents and seal went into a leather satchel, the whole package ready within a day of Natalie receiving the note. She couldn't possibly deposit it in the designated place so quickly, however. It would only raise suspicions if she acted too quickly. If she were truly planning to steal such confidential items, she would need time to manage the feat.

It was also in her own interests to wait to place the satchel until close to the blackmailer's deadline. Once she'd put it in position, she would need to watch the spot day and night in order to ensure she was there to see it collected.

Sitting on her hands and doing nothing had never been Natalie's strong suit, however. Surely the blackmailer would check the cache periodically rather than waiting until the end of the window he had given her. He would want to be less predictable than that. So placing it early wouldn't necessarily mean waiting for days. He was probably checking at least once a day.

Rising early one morning, Natalie's patience snapped. She couldn't bear any more time spent alone and waiting. But she wasn't even halfway to the designated place, deep in the palace gardens, when a cheerful voice hailed her by name. She ground her teeth together as she turned to face Luca.

He had to be watching her, given he managed to appear at all the most inopportune times.

"What do you want now?" she asked. "If you're here to drag me off to another empty social event, I'm not going. Not today."

"Perfect," he said with a grin. "Since I'm not going today either."

She finally absorbed his appearance and blinked. She had never seen him less than impeccably dressed, as most Lanoverians tended to be. But today only his air of confidence and his possession of the royal jawline distinguished him from a farm laborer.

"What are you wearing?" she asked, completely distracted.

"Something practical. But I brought a coverall for you." He held out a long length of heavy material.

"For me?" She stared at him blankly. "What are you talking about?"

"Today we're doing something a little less empty," he said. "Unless you'd rather go and make small talk…"

He waited, eyebrow raised in challenge.

Curiosity burned in Natalie like fire. She glanced down at her satchel and then back at him. It wasn't as if she could go and deliver it as planned if Luca was going to trail along behind her.

He called toward the palace, and a footman appeared, jogging to meet them.

"Put the princess's bag in her room," he instructed the man, gesturing for Natalie to hand over her satchel.

She hesitated. But refusing to hand it over would only draw Luca's attention to it. Reluctantly she unslung it from her shoulder and passed it to the waiting footman, her eyes following him as he headed back toward the palace.

"Stop fretting." Luca handed her the coverall he'd been holding. "He'll see it safely to your room."

She put on the length of material, pleased to see that it covered her dress without dragging awkwardly on the ground. He'd judged her size and height well.

"Where are we going?" she asked as he led her across the garden toward an area she hadn't yet visited. "And are you really allowed to be seen like that?"

"Encouraged, even." He gave a languid grin. "Lanover has always been less formal than the northern kingdoms. It's the heat."

She gave him a suspicious look, but he appeared to be serious.

"Casual enough that royal princes take secondary jobs as hired hands?"

He laughed. "Not quite. But the people like to see the royal family pitching in and getting their hands dirty from time to time. And my job of choice has always been the orange harvest. I'm a quick hand at orange picking, if I say so myself."

Natalie followed his gaze to where a small orchard

occupied one corner of the vast palace grounds. It was tucked away behind a freestanding building that she guessed to be some sort of servants' quarters.

Luca led her past the building into the first rows of trees. The scent of apple blossoms surrounded her, and she stopped to admire the beauty of the blooms. But Luca kept walking, going deeper into the orchard, past the apple trees, and she ran to catch up.

"It's the last harvest for the oranges for this year," he said, "so I couldn't miss the opportunity."

"And you thought I would want to join in?" She said the words with a faintly mocking lilt, but he just smiled at her.

"Wouldn't you?"

She hesitated, not wanting to admit that he'd judged her correctly. But after a moment she laughed and nodded. Fair was fair.

The workers already spread along the rows of orange trees called greetings to Luca. They addressed him as Your Highness but didn't stop in their picking for any other formalities. All of them wore large canvas bags, secured with wide straps to their waist or shoulders, and Luca retrieved two more bags from a pile beside the first tree.

He helped Natalie settle one across her shoulders and led her toward a tree laden with bright orange fruit. A simple wooden ladder leaned against the branches, and she eyed it dubiously.

"Don't worry," Luca said. "It's your first time picking, so you can stay on the ground. We'll work on the same tree—you can do the lower branches while I do the upper ones."

"So I just…pick them?" Natalie asked.

Luca easily scaled the ladder, pulling an orange from its

stem and dropping it into his bag. "Just like that! It's easy! The hard part is getting anywhere near the speed of the professional pickers."

He began to pick oranges so fast Natalie could barely follow his hands. Her eyes widened as she watched him, his head bare and his expression carefree as his hands flashed through the leaves. He was mesmerizing to watch.

But when he glanced down at her and raised an eyebrow, she hurriedly took hold of the closest fruit. It twisted easily off its stem, and she dropped it into the bag. Thankfully the canvas receptacle was large enough that its bottom rested on the ground, taking the weight of the oranges. She picked another and another, starting to get a rhythm going, although she was far from Luca's speed.

"Leo and I used to have competitions when we were young to see who could pick the most oranges in a set amount of time." He continued working as he spoke, raising his voice just enough that she could catch his words. "I always won, of course." He winked down at her, and she rolled her eyes.

"I'm sure." She picked several more oranges. "And I'm equally sure that if Leo was telling the story, his memory would be that he always won." She shook her head at the exploits of small boys. Some things didn't change between kingdoms. "I never had oranges growing up. I didn't taste my first one until I was fourteen."

Luca looked down at her in surprise. "Why ever not?"

Natalie nearly explained that the mountain kingdom didn't grow them, so she hadn't even seen one until the mountain passes were first opened, reconnecting her people with the rest of the kingdoms. But the words died in her throat as she realized her mistake. She was growing far too comfortable around Luca.

"I just…didn't," she said, knowing her words sounded strange and cold.

His brow furrowed, but he didn't challenge her, returning to his work picking oranges instead.

"Well, you're welcome to as many as you'd like while you're here in Lanover," he said. "As you can see, the royal family has plenty."

"Are these all for the palace, then?" Natalie asked, amazed.

Luca shrugged. "Have you seen how many people live and work at the palace? You'd be surprised how quickly they go."

They continued to chat as they worked, Natalie keeping a careful guard over her tongue to prevent further mistakes. It was hard to remember her assumed role while they worked side by side. For once, Luca seemed no more like a prince than she was a princess. But she would be wise to remember that for one of them it was only an illusion, while for the other it was a reality she would soon return to.

# CHAPTER 12

The orange picking had taken all day, and she and Luca had joined the other workers for the evening meal at the end of it. Everyone had been in the kind of good spirits that only come from enjoying hearty food at the end of a satisfying day's work. Your muscles might ache, but it was the kind of ache that reminded you you'd earned the chance to sit down and eat well.

Natalie had intended to make a second attempt at depositing the satchel the next day. But one of the girls from the orange picking had told her about a famous seamstress in the city who made gowns of unusual design and material. The girl only worked seasonally at the palace and did odd jobs for the seamstress in the other months, and she would be returning to the city now that the last of the orange trees had been stripped. She offered to introduce Natalie to Reya, the seamstress, and even negotiate a discount on a commission for her.

Luca caught the interested gleam in Natalie's eyes and promised to escort her to the city the next day. True to his word, he showed up at her chamber door promptly the next morning, ready for their excursion.

Natalie went with him willingly since there was no rush to deposit the satchel. In fact, it had been impatience that had driven her there so early in the first place, so any distraction was a good thing.

She told herself the same thing the next day and the next. Given her official role, she still had to attend most court functions, but in between events, Luca helped her explore the capital.

She knew he was monitoring her. Every now and then she caught his eyes on her with the same questioning look she had seen before. But if he was using the chance to try to discover her secrets, she was using it to distract them both—him from her secret plans and herself from placing the satchel too early.

And she couldn't deny her relief at having something to do beyond the dry royal functions. Luca was as clearly bored by them as she was, and something had changed between them since the orange picking. He still laughed and teased, but she no longer felt like he was laughing at her, or that she was playing the losing hand in a game she didn't understand.

But the days—now full of interesting new experiences —slipped by far too easily. Natalie forgot she was merely counting down time, and it was with a jolt that she realized she had reached the final day of the blackmailer's deadline.

Returning from the city in a rush to change for the evening meal, she had tumbled into her room and happened to notice the satchel, half tucked behind her dressing table. Her eyes flew to the window where dusk was already falling.

"Never mind the dress!" she cried to Donna, who was holding an evening gown toward her. "I have to go!"

She seized the satchel and fled back into the corridor. As she rushed toward the gardens, she berated herself silently. What had she been thinking? How had she let herself lose sight of what mattered?

"It's all Luca's fault!" she muttered as she stepped outside. But even as she said the words, she knew her true anger was directed at herself.

Had she been too clever when she had instructed the princes to call her by her own pet name? It was like she had forgotten she wasn't really Princess Rose, and it wasn't really her life she was living. She had kept the role in order to fool the blackmailer—only to then forget all about depositing the satchel!

Berating herself, she hurried through the gardens. But once again she only made it partway before a familiar voice called her name.

She spun, anger still pulsing through her, to see Luca smiling in friendly greeting. They had parted less than twenty minutes earlier, but he was already dressed in finery for the planned formal dinner.

His smile fell away as he took in her expression, concern taking its place. He stepped hurriedly toward her.

"Lila, what's wrong? Did something happen?"

The sight of him unleashed such a mass of conflicting feelings that she exploded.

"What are you doing here? Are you following me?"

"Following you?" He looked confused. "No, of course not."

"Do you really expect me to believe that? Every time I turn around, you're there! I can't move without tripping over you."

Something that might have been pain flashed in his eyes, and her insides twisted in response. But she could hear a clock ticking down in her head, reminding her that she couldn't afford to let Luca distract her yet again.

He stepped even closer—so close his jacket brushed against her arm.

"Something's going on. I know it is. I just wish you would trust me. I can help you."

But the time for talking was long past. She needed to get rid of him. Frustration and fear coiled within her as the clock continued to tick. She lashed out.

"Trust you? Do you think I don't know you were instructed to occupy me—to distract me and keep me out of your precious cousin's way?"

He froze, his expression turning wary, and she knew her suspicions were right. Distantly she wondered why Leo had wanted to avoid the Arcadian princess, but that didn't matter now either.

Luca was still standing far too close. Her thoughts swirled chaotically, and the clock continued to relentlessly tick.

She waited for him to step back, to admit the truth of her words and apologize. To give her space to breathe now that she had exposed his game.

But instead, he stepped even closer, grasping her upper arms in a firm grip and gazing down into her face.

"Did it work?" His voice was deep and rough. "Are you distracted?"

They were both breathing hard, locked together, far too close. She couldn't break her gaze free of the fire in his, any more than she could step back and break the contact between them. She was trapped in the moment, unable to do anything but answer honestly.

"Yes," she whispered, and the flames between them ignited.

He pulled her against him, their lips connecting as she rose to meet him, swept away in the moment. All their tension, suspicion, and laughter turned to fire as he deepened the kiss.

She had been pretending she wasn't attracted to him since their first meeting, but there was no longer any pretense between them. Only passion remained.

And then she remembered it was only an illusion. Pretense remained at the heart of every one of their interactions. He had only sought her out because he believed she was Princess Rose.

She pulled out of his arms, gasping, her eyes wide.

His hands fell to his sides, his face going white as he stared at her, chest heaving.

"I didn't mean to do that." His voice came out flat with shock. "Not when—"

Natalie didn't wait to hear the rest. It had been a mistake on her side, and now he had confirmed it had been a mistake for him as well. If she left now—if they never spoke of it again—they could pretend it had never happened.

She fled straight back to her room. Bursting through

the door, she shouted for the maids to get out, and they left in a flurry of wide eyes and shocked whispers. Natalie collapsed on the bed, but this time she didn't cry. She couldn't even think. She just lay there, mind blank.

But while she couldn't form words, she could still feel. Feel Luca's lips burning on hers. Feel his fingers wrapping around her arms and pulling her against him.

And she could hear a lone whisper growing from the back of her mind.

*She was never going to forget that kiss.*

The last remnants of the light faded, plunging the room into darkness. In the absence of the maids, the candles remained unlit, and the dark around her pressed in on Natalie's awareness. The strap of the satchel pulled against her neck, uncomfortable where it had twisted beneath her as she flopped on the bed.

She sat up abruptly. What was the time?

How could she have forgotten her mission *again*? The note had said midnight. Surely she still had time to get the satchel in place before then.

She left the room at a sprint, taking nothing but the satchel. A lantern would have been helpful for the dark garden paths, but she couldn't risk being seen and stopped yet again—not by Luca or anyone. It was her last chance.

Passing beneath a dense patch of foliage, she lost sight of the path and tripped on an uneven patch of gravel. She fell hard, sprawling across the path. But she scrambled to her feet again within seconds. Skinned hands and torn dresses didn't matter. The only thing that mattered was reaching the exchange location in time.

She arrived out of breath, trembling from the exertion. There was no time to pause, however. She slid the satchel beneath the rusted iron bench seat—an anomaly in the otherwise well tended garden. Apparently it had been forgotten, left to age in this far corner of the garden. How had the blackmailer stumbled on it and known it would be a safe place to leave the documents and seal?

Natalie considered the question as she concealed herself behind the largest bush she could find. The blackmailer must have spent time in the palace grounds. But with no walls between the palace and the city, there would be no records of who frequented the gardens. He had likely chosen the locations for her convenience, knowing that he could easily slip in unnoticed, whereas her departure from the palace grounds would be likely to arouse interest.

She fought to reclaim her breath after her wild run, her heartbeat gradually slowing. She had made it. Without much time to spare, but she had made it.

Was the blackmailer already concealed nearby? Had he seen her arrive and then hide behind the bush?

She examined her surroundings, but it was hard to see much in the dimness of night. In all her strategizing, it hadn't occurred to her that he might plan to wait and watch just as she was planning to do. But it was too late to worry about it now.

She waited. The silent, still minutes contrasted strangely with her earlier frantic haste. She had no idea of the exact time, but at least two hours must have passed before her eyes caught a flicker of light.

She rose to her knees, eyes peering through the leaves. Someone was approaching.

A thin stream of light illuminated a small patch of gravel path. The person moving toward her had shuttered their lantern—directing its light into a single, focused beam. The blackmailer. It had to be. A palace resident or guard on patrol wouldn't take measures not to be seen.

Natalie's mind focused to a single point. She had been given a second chance to follow the man, and she couldn't waste it. She would have to use every sense she possessed because she couldn't afford to stumble or trip in the darkness as she had earlier.

As far as she could tell, the man appeared to be the same one who had come to the gazebo. He had once again covered himself from head to toe, and he looked around carefully before stooping and retrieving the satchel. Resting it on the bench, he extracted the pile of documents from inside.

Natalie held her breath. This was the moment that would determine the success or failure of her ruse. If he gave them more than a cursory glance…

He looked up, responding to a distant noise, and she wanted to cheer. He was going to take the satchel and leave. He was—

He turned back to the documents, his eyes skimming over the top one. A crease grew on his forehead, illuminated in the light of his lantern. He turned to the next paper and skimmed it even more quickly before shoving the whole pile back in the satchel.

Natalie held her breath, relieved he hadn't thrown the papers away. But his face showed his suspicion as he pulled out the tiny leather pouch with the seal. If he opened it and examined the contents closely…

He tipped the seal onto his palm and held it toward the light.

His growl of fury made Natalie swallow and back slowly away behind her screen of greenery. Her careful plan now looked foolish and thin. How could she have thought it would succeed?

What would the man do now? Had Natalie wrecked everything?

She should have talked to Rose. She should have found out what was at stake rather than blithely trusting in her own ability to handle the situation. What if she'd brought disaster to the princess or to Arcadia?

She had been so confident, so full of her success during the mountain kingdom rebellion. But she hadn't stopped to think about the differences between then and now. At home, she had been operating in familiar territory, and she hadn't been acting alone. She had overestimated her abilities, and she might not be the only one to pay the price.

She gulped and moved further back. One of her arms brushed against another bush, making an audible rustle. The man's head shot up, swinging in her direction.

For a second she stayed frozen in place, not even breathing, hoping he would dismiss it as a breeze or a small nighttime animal. But he dropped the satchel and its contents and bounded toward her.

Natalie leaped to her feet, fleeing toward the closest path. But just as she reached it, her foot caught in a trailing loop of her dress—a tear left from her earlier fall. Crashing to the ground, the man was on her before she could rise again.

He seized her hands and hauled her roughly upward, twisting her so the lantern light fell on her face.

"You're not Princess Rose!" he growled. "Where is she? What are you doing here?"

Faced with the moment of crisis, Natalie's fear faded, her mind racing for a way out of the situation.

"I'm her lady-in-waiting." Her dress was too expensive to claim she was only a maid. "The princess sent me in her place. She couldn't possibly go sneaking around the gardens at night herself!" She tried to sound prim and foolish.

The man shook her, his eyes hardening. "And do you know your mistress sent you to play a trick? Of course she wouldn't come into harm's way herself when she was planning such a thing. But apparently she didn't care about your fate. How like a princess."

"Princess Rose cares!" Natalie cried indignantly.

The man chuckled, and Natalie realized her mistake.

"Does she, indeed? How convenient. We will see just how much she cares when her lady fails to return to her. We'll see if she cares about the price you must pay for her twice failure."

He meant to kidnap her? Natalie didn't have to fake the fear on her face. But beneath her anxiety, her mind was still working. If he took her to his base, she could still salvage the situation. Once she was there, she could—

He pulled out a knife.

White hot terror lanced through her. He meant to murder her?

She thrashed, fighting with every ounce of desperation she possessed to escape his grip. Her sudden, frenzied movement took him by surprise, and she succeeded in breaking free. Staggering sideways, she yanked up her skirts to run.

But she was too slow. He pounced on her, seizing her hair and using it to drag her backward. She screamed—unleashing all her pain, fear, and outrage. She refused to be murdered so easily.

"Lila?" a voice shouted in response to her cry.

Running footsteps pounded against gravel somewhere nearby. Natalie went limp with relief. Once again, Luca had turned up where he wasn't supposed to be, and she had never been so glad of anything.

Her assailant cursed and hesitated, apparently gripped by indecision. Natalie seized her hair in both hands and yanked it free of his grip, staggering away from him.

He moved to follow her, but Luca's running footsteps were getting closer. The man's eyes jumped to something over her shoulder, and he stopped.

She didn't turn to look herself, however. Lunging forward, she seized the material around his head, pulling it free and exposing his face.

He cursed again, his arm jumping up to cover his exposed features as he turned to flee.

Luca's running footsteps had nearly reached her, and Natalie collapsed to the ground, her knees wobbly with relief. Luca was already sprinting at full speed, and the blackmailer had almost no head start. The prince would easily run him down.

But as Luca came into view, a drawn sword in his hand,

he swerved, coming to her side instead of running after the man.

"Lila!" He dropped to one knee beside her, wrapping his free arm around her shoulders. "Are you all right? Where are you hurt?"

"I'm not hurt!" She ignored the stinging in her scalp from the violent tugs to her hair. "What are you doing? Catch him!"

But Luca didn't move. "I'm not leaving you alone."

"Forget about me!" Natalie cried, seething with frustration. "You need to catch him!"

Luca's face took on a stubborn cast, and he made no move to leave her side. Gently he helped her to her feet.

"I didn't get a good look at his face," Luca said, "but he had a knife. There's no way I'm leaving you alone."

"Of course he had a knife! He was trying to murder me!"

"Murder you? Are you saying that man was an assassin?" Luca's eyes scanned the nearby garden, his sword rising back into position. "Why would an assassin come to the Lanoverian palace to kill the princess of Arcadia?"

Natalie was almost crying in frustration. "Of course he wasn't here to kill Princess Rose! I'm not—"

She clapped her hand over her mouth, horror filling her. Her feet stepped away from him, every instinct telling her to run and hide. But she couldn't tear her eyes away from Luca's.

He stared back at her, the supposed assassin forgotten, his concern and outrage replaced with blank shock.

# CHAPTER 14

"You're not Princess Rose," Luca said slowly, his shock already fading into something she couldn't read.

Natalie's hand dropped from her mouth, but she said nothing, waiting to see what he would do next.

"If you're not Princess Rose, then who are you?" he asked matter-of-factly.

"I'm Natalie, of course. Nata*lie—Li*la. Lila really is my childhood nickname."

"Natalie," he said softly, a small smile playing at the edges of his mouth. "I should have seen that."

"You're not angry?" Natalie asked, unable to help herself. He was taking it so calmly.

He tipped his head to the side, as if considering the matter. "I think I am—a little. But it's also a relief to finally make sense of everything." One side of his mouth curved up. "Like why you hadn't tasted an orange until you were fourteen. That was when the mountain passes opened, I assume?"

She nodded her head silently.

"And if you're Natalie," he continued, puzzling it out for himself, "then I presume the Natalie I know is actually Princess Rose?"

Natalie nodded again and then added in a rush, "I didn't force her to switch! She suggested it."

Luca raised an eyebrow, but he didn't dispute the statement. "She certainly seems to be enjoying herself playing mountain girl. And this whole time…" He suddenly tipped his head back and laughed loudly.

Natalie watched him in bewilderment. She couldn't see any amusement in the situation herself. Not only had she accidentally revealed her secrets, but they hadn't even caught the man threatening Rose.

Luca's laughter subsided into chuckles. "This whole time…" He shook his head. "I wonder what he'll do now?"

"Who?" Natalie's patience was fraying along with her nerves. "What are you talking about?"

"Never mind." Luca's attention switched abruptly back to her. "I'm much more interested in what we're going to do."

"What do you mean?" Natalie asked, wary again.

"If that wasn't an assassin trying to kill Princess Rose, then it was someone trying to kill you. Why was someone trying to kill you, Lila?"

"Oh, that."

"Yes," he said wryly. "That."

"He recognized I wasn't the princess, so I told him I was Princess Rose's lady-in-waiting. He was going to kill me in order to punish her and send her a message."

Luca's hand tightened on the hilt of his sword. "He was going to…"

Words seemed to fail him, and Natalie sighed. Now he looked ready to dash off after her attacker. Where was that outrage when it could have been helpful?

Luca gestured toward the bench where she'd hidden the satchel. "I think we should sit down because I need to hear everything from the beginning. And I get the feeling it's going to be a long story."

He took her arm firmly, guiding her toward the seat. But he paused before sitting. "Unless we should be worried about a fresh wave of attackers arriving at any moment?"

Natalie shook her head. "I don't think so. As far as I know, it's just one man, and I think you effectively scared him away."

Luca nodded and gently pushed her onto the seat. He took the time to retrieve the abandoned lantern, removing the shutters before sitting beside her. The fresh illumination revealed the determined lines of his face. He was clearly going to insist on hearing everything before he let her escape to her room.

Her shoulders slumped. She'd been fooling him for weeks, so she had to admit he had the right to demand answers.

"Rose and I traveled here together," she said, starting at the beginning, as she'd been instructed. "Just the two of us. That's when we came up with the idea to switch places."

"It's incredible you got away with it," he said. "It never would have worked if the whole court was here."

"We wouldn't even have attempted it except for the

tour. Rose was certain that everyone she knew would be traveling with your parents."

"You said it was Princess Rose's suggestion? What reason could she have to want to live your life?"

"I think it was more that she didn't want to live hers—just for a little." Natalie peeked at him warily. How much could she safely say? "She was feeling a little...pressured. About certain *expectations*."

"About Leo, you mean?" He went off into fresh gales of laughter.

Once again, he made no attempt to explain his merriment, merely wiping his eyes and gesturing for her to continue.

"We were expecting the crown prince to be dancing attendance on Princess Rose, and it suited us both for him to spend that time with me instead of her." Natalie wrinkled her nose. "Not that it worked out anything like we expected."

Luca fixed her with a stern expression, all trace of laughter extinguished. Natalie winced, but she was sick of half-truths and careful concealments. If Luca hated her once he knew the full truth, that was his right.

"I came to Lanover to marry Prince Leo," she said in a rush. "So I could eventually become a queen, like Gwen and Charlotte."

His eyes narrowed, but he looked more triumphant than horrified. "I knew it! Right from the beginning I questioned your motives. I could tell you were hiding something. Leo thought I was imagining it, but I was so certain."

Despite her guilt and contrition, Natalie felt the stirrings of indignation.

"It didn't stop you kissing me!"

Her accusation sobered him instantly.

"As I said at the time, that was a mistake."

The repetition of his earlier words hit her in the chest like a blow.

But he continued without pause, his expression rueful. "As much as I'd been wanting to kiss you, I was determined not to do so until I knew what you were hiding from me. But I lost control for a moment, and..." He gave her a boyish grin. "Sorry about that."

Her mind went blank. He'd been wanting to kiss her even before that? For how long?

She wanted to demand answers, but she couldn't do that until she'd taken responsibility for her mistakes.

"I'm the one who should be sorry," she said. "The whole scheme was outrageous—I can see that now. When Gwen took the throne in the mountain kingdom, my parents shut me out of court. After everything I'd done to help the rebellion, I felt betrayed. I thought the answer was to become someone so important that no one could ever shut me out again. I thought that way I could become the kind of person who mattered—who did things that mattered. But I never properly considered Leo in the middle of all that. Looking back now, I was painfully naïve. I didn't think of it as using him. I was so sure that I'd arrive, and Leo and I would just...just fall in love."

"We are a good-looking family," Luca said with a grin that made her glare at him.

His expression softened, and he took her hand. "You don't need to marry Leo to matter, Lila. I hope you know that."

Natalie grimaced. "I just hope your cousin won't take offense on behalf of Lanover. We initially only planned to switch for a few days, and I actually thought he'd already have fallen in love with me by then." She gave a pained laugh. "I was sure he'd forgive everything when we confessed the truth. But everything has spiraled out of control, and I'm terrified my foolish naïveté is going to cause an international incident." She gave Luca a worried look. "Maybe we shouldn't mention my reasons for the switch to Leo?"

"Maybe not," he agreed solemnly, but he looked like he was once again struggling not to laugh at something she didn't understand.

"I'm still surprised the princess was willing to take the risk," he said after a moment of silence. "She should have known better."

"When we discussed it, we thought it sounded like something the two of you would have done," Natalie explained. "So we thought you'd have to forgive us."

This time he did break out into laughter.

"We might have switched places a time or two when we were younger," he admitted once his fresh mirth subsided.

"Does that mean you'll forgive me for the deception?" Natalie asked in a small voice. "I truly regret it."

"I don't regret it at all," he said promptly.

Her eyes flew to his. He was smiling, but his eyes were focused on the dark depths of the garden, his thoughts seemingly elsewhere. "It might have done a great deal of good."

She waited, but he let the thought drop, turning to her with a twinkle. "Having confessed my own disgraceful past, I can hardly refuse to forgive you without making myself a hypocrite."

Natalie bit her lip, not wanting to grow too hopeful. "You're not upset that I'm not really a princess?"

He raised an eyebrow. "I think we've already covered the reprehensible nature of pursuing someone only for their rank. I may be a prince, but I believe the same principle applies. On the matter of your true identity, at least, we can make peace."

Relief swept over Natalie, but she didn't have time to enjoy it before his voice turned darker.

"There is, however, another matter. Your misguided swap with Princess Rose does not explain why I just found a masked man trying to stab you in the palace gardens."

"That has nothing to do with the swap," Natalie said. "At least not initially." She explained her discovery of the note on Rose's pillow and everything that had happened since, concluding with, "So you can see why I got so annoyed at you when you kept getting in the way."

"See why *you* were annoyed with *me*?" Luca looked up from examining the two notes, gathering wrath in his eyes. "See that you were determined to get yourself killed, more like! Of all the misguided, foolish, mule-headed—"

"Don't!" Natalie put up a hand to stop the rush of words, tears pricking at her eyes.

"I know it was foolish of me. I've realized that already. I'll let Rose lecture me all she wants, but not you. There's been no harm done to Lanover."

"No harm to..." He twisted his body toward her, grasping her arm and staring down at her. "Do you think

I'm worried about Lanover? You could have been killed! If I hadn't heard you scream, you would have been!"

"Yes, that was very timely of you!" Natalie said, distracted by his words. "How did you manage to be on hand so quickly?"

"Timely." He let out a breath, running a hand through his hair. "Do you have any idea how long I was searching? One of the servants told me she'd seen you dashing outside like you had wolves on your heels, and I went straight after you. I was searching for you all evening." He fixed her with a direct look. "Did you think I was going to let you run away after that kiss?"

"Oh." Natalie hung her head, her cheeks flushing.

"Yes," he said. "Oh."

He took one of her hands in both of his, holding it in a grip that was both warm and reassuring. His voice gentled as he spoke, drawing her eyes back to his.

"It was foolish of you to keep the notes secret and try to handle it yourself, but it was also brave. You were trying to protect Rose, and that at least, can be commended."

Her flush deepened, but then he kept talking. "If you'd only told me when I repeatedly asked you what was going on. We could have had this place teeming with guards."

She pulled her hand free and threw it in the air. "And you wonder that I didn't want to tell you! That would have been a terrible idea! The blackmailer was canny enough to notice one girl hiding in the bushes. You would have scared him off before he ever got close." She shook her head. "At least this time wasn't a total disaster like last time. I managed to get a look at his face before he ran off."

"Not a total disaster? Are you serious?" He stared at her. "He came within a breath of stabbing you!"

"But he didn't," she said, indisputably.

"Only because I arrived just in time!"

"I wouldn't have been here at all if you hadn't come blundering along and scared him off the first time!"

He groaned in frustration. "I wouldn't have blundered anywhere if you'd just included me from the beginning."

Natalie gave a laugh that ended on a sigh. "Honestly, I'm surprised I managed to fool everyone this long. I'm sure Rose is much too well bred to argue with a prince." She stood.

Luca stood as well. "Maybe this prince prefers honest arguments to polite manners."

Natalie laughed. "Very prettily said, Your Highness. But it's been a long night, and I'm too tired for either arguments or manners. I'm going to bed."

"I'll escort you back to the palace," he said in a voice that brooked no argument.

She had no desire to argue. After escaping her attacker by such a narrow margin, she was grateful for Luca's armed presence at her side as she walked back through the dark gardens. She would have been jumping at every rustle and shadow otherwise.

"Are you really going to start calling me Your Highness?" he asked as they walked. "We've already agreed to use our first names."

"That was an agreement you made with Princess Rose," Natalie said.

Luca shook his head. "No. Everything I said was to *you*,

not to your supposed title. Believe me, I didn't plan for any of what happened between us."

Natalie said nothing, unsure how to take his words.

"I still intend to call you Lila," he said quietly, glancing at her sideways as if he hoped his words might goad her into speech.

But she still didn't say anything. She was too tired to sort through all her conflicting thoughts and emotions.

He sighed and turned the topic of conversation in a different direction. "Princess Rose isn't going to thank us if she loses her chance to recover the Arcadian seal over this."

"Arcadian seal?" Natalie asked. "What seal?"

"Didn't you know?" He looked at her in surprise. "That's what the blackmailer was referring to in his notes. Leo told me about it weeks ago. A thief managed to steal a number of important documents from Arcadia, along with an official seal. It all happened before you got here."

"Those were the same items he wanted from Lanover!" Natalie exclaimed.

Luca nodded, giving her an odd look. "Didn't you notice the seal he used on the letters he sent you? It was the Arcadian royal seal. He used it to authenticate his identity as the thief. I suppose his theft had worked so well the first time, he decided to try it again with Lanover."

Natalie felt foolish. "I've never seen the Arcadian seal before. I didn't give the one on the notes much thought."

"You've at least heard of the spymaster Aurora, I assume?" Luca asked.

Natalie nodded. Everyone had heard of Aurora.

"Her spy network tracked the thief as far as Lanover, and they've been working to identify him ever since. So while I agree that a squad of guards would have given the game away, Leo could have posted spies to watch for the blackmailer."

Natalie bit her lip. That definitely would have been a better strategy than her trying to watch on her own.

"The thief is obviously unaware that your family already knows about his past theft," she mused. "He was obviously expecting Rose to keep the loss a secret rather than going to Leo for help."

"The Arcadians have kept it quiet," Luca said. "Aurora told Father about it directly."

"Aurora?" Natalie raised her brows. "I thought she worked for all the Four Kingdoms. Is she in the habit of telling Arcadia's secrets to Lanover? And does Arcadia know about that?"

"She only tells us the secrets she thinks we really need to know." Luca sounded amused. "I've overheard some heated conversations about it. Given she's their sister, Father and Uncle Frederic think she should tell them more. But she insists that she works for the good of all the kingdoms now. She just sometimes thinks the good of the kingdoms requires fewer secrets."

"That's rich coming from a spymaster," Natalie said, and Luca laughed.

"That's exactly what Father said. He's just sore that she's the queen of Northhelm now, so Northhelm knows all the secrets." Luca looked sideways at her. "You know we have to tell Rose and Leo everything, right? And you two need to swap back. Our parents will be back from their tour soon. You can't keep up the charade."

"I've been wanting to swap back since our first night,"

she said. "Only the blackmailing situation made me continue the ruse." She hesitated. "But can you let me talk to Rose first? I can't start making grand announcements without giving her any warning. I'll find her first thing in the morning."

Luca sighed. "I suppose that's reasonable. And while you're talking to her, I'll talk to the guards—see if anyone has seen anything suspicious. If nothing else, I want to find out how he managed to leave secret notes on your pillow!"

"I'd be interested to know that myself," Natalie said absently, her thoughts on her upcoming conversation with Rose. Would the princess be angry that she'd told Luca everything?

She was more likely to be angry at Natalie's mishandling of the blackmailer. Natalie winced. One way or another, it wasn't going to be an enjoyable conversation.

But she would do everything in her power to help Rose find the man and recover Arcadia's seal. Natalie had seen his face, at least, so she might be able to give some actual assistance. And it sounded as if the Lanoverian princes were willing to help as well. Between them all, there had to be a way.

# CHAPTER 15

Natalie went to Rose's room to talk to her before breakfast the next morning. But the princess was already gone, leaving Joanne to clean up the remains of her meal.

"Where's Rose?" she asked the maid.

"I'm not sure." Joanne looked concerned. "She's been extremely busy lately, but she won't tell me what she's so busy with. I heard someone talking about a series of meetings, but that doesn't make much sense…"

Natalie left, a furrow between her brows. What sort of meetings could Rose possibly be attending as Natalie? Natalie could make no more sense of it than Joanne. And she could hardly search the whole palace room by room.

At least Joanne had promised to inform Rose that Natalie was looking for her. And Natalie could stop by her room again later in the day.

But despite visiting the room twice more, Natalie had no success in locating Rose. After the third attempt, she returned to her own room, dispirited. Where could Rose be?

Hilary, Donna, and Cate ambushed her as soon as she was inside, locking the door behind her and fixing her with identical stern looks.

"There's a royal ball tonight," Donna said, firmly seating her at the dressing table and beginning to arrange her hair. "It's the final event of the season and is being held in honor of the Arcadian princess. Her Highness left us strict instructions that you will not be allowed to disgrace Arcadia by turning up looking bedraggled—or not turning up at all."

Natalie meekly submitted, guiltily aware of the events she had missed in the last couple of weeks. Given Rose's own absence, Natalie hadn't realized the Arcadian had noticed.

"I really do need to speak to Princess Rose. Urgently." Natalie met Donna's eyes in the mirror. "Do you really not know where she can be found? None of you?"

"We have our suspicions," Cate said with a giggle, but Donna shushed her.

"Right now she'll be in her own room with Joanne, preparing for the ball," Hilary said with confidence.

Natalie started up, but Donna pushed her firmly back down. "You'll both be at the ball soon enough. If you're so desperate to talk to her, you can do it then."

Natalie winced. A crowded ballroom wasn't the ideal location for a private conversation. But perhaps they could steal out into the garden for a few minutes.

Memories of the blackmailer and his knife flashed

through her mind. She shivered. Just not too far into the gardens.

She didn't protest again as the maids dressed her in a filmy lilac gown with a lace bodice. It had always been a favorite of hers, and when they placed Rose's golden circlet in her hair, she surveyed her appearance in the room's full-length mirror. She couldn't find a fault. Based on her appearance alone, she really could have been a queen.

The illusion continued as she stood at the top of the shallow steps leading down into the ballroom, a fanfare sounding to announce her arrival. All eyes turned to her, and she had to fight not to shudder. Had this really been the dream she had cherished for three years?

Her ambitions seemed distant and foolish now, all her thoughts on finding Rose—and avoiding Luca until she'd done so. He'd want to know if she'd talked to Rose yet, and she didn't think he'd be impressed to hear they'd both been too busy preparing for the ball.

Natalie prowled up and down the ballroom, avoiding any men who tried to approach her. She wasn't in the mood for dancing with random courtiers. She didn't even stop at the refreshment table, or step outside to examine the decorative lanterns that lit up the nearest stretch of garden. But despite her efforts, she managed only one glimpse of Rose as she flashed past on the dance floor before being immediately lost among the whirling dancers again.

Twice she spotted Luca moving determinedly in her direction and had to dodge through the crowd. If the dancers didn't disperse soon, she was going to run out of places to hide.

The music finally ended, and Natalie pushed through the wave of bodies leaving the dance floor, searching for Rose among the throng. She turned left and caught sight of Luca, her eyes catching his before she could turn away. She swerved abruptly right, bent on escape, and walked straight into Prince Leo.

He steadied her with a hand on her elbow. "Princess Rose." He sounded oddly formal. "I'm glad to see you."

"You are?" Natalie asked, too distracted to consider her words. Given the way he'd been avoiding her since her arrival in Lanover, she couldn't imagine why he would be looking for her now.

He shifted uncomfortably as the strains of the next song began. Glancing around at their position in the middle of the dance floor, he said quickly, "Dance with me."

"I—" She looked over his shoulder, still searching for Rose. But he was the crown prince, and the dance was already beginning. Who knew what rumors she'd start if she conspicuously rejected him in the middle of the dance floor? "Very well." She put her hand in his and let him sweep her into the dance.

He danced well, leading with confidence. But Natalie felt none of the fire she had felt when she circled the room in Luca's arms. From the first moment, she had responded differently to Luca than to his cousin.

She shook her head at her own past foolishness. How could she have thought the heart was so easily bidden?

She tried to look for Rose as they circled, but they were twirling too quickly. Instead of Rose, her eyes locked on

Luca. Her stomach twisted at the hurt on his face. Surely he didn't think she was still chasing after his cousin?

Leo cleared his throat, and Natalie remembered she should be speaking. Did he find their silence odd? But he wasn't making an effort to speak either. The entire dance was growing more awkward by the minute.

Their movements took them near the edge of the dance floor, beside one of the long windows that gave access to the gardens. Leo didn't turn them back toward the other dancers, instead spinning her all the way to the edge of the room. He paused there, his hand dropping from her waist.

"Would you mind walking with me a moment, Your Highness?"

Natalie's eyebrows rose. Your Highness? He was back to the formality.

She looked over her shoulder, still searching for Rose, but she couldn't think of a reason to refuse to speak to Leo.

"If you like...Your Highness," she quickly added, remembering to match his tone.

He led her outside, his stern expression discouraging anyone from approaching them. They were soon alone, close enough to the ball that they remained within the light of the decorative lanterns, but with no one in earshot.

"I realize I should have spoken to you sooner," Leo said, still in the same stilted, formal tones.

Panic clawed at Natalie. Had Luca already spoken to him? What had he said about her?

"I'm aware that our parents had certain hopes for this visit," Leo continued, "and that you may have come here with certain expectations yourself. I shouldn't have waited so long to clarify my position, and I hope I haven't caused any pain on your end. While I value Lanover's alliance with Arcadia, I have no intentions of pursuing a marriage alliance with you now or ever."

Natalie blinked. That's what he wanted to talk to her about? She could have laughed.

Nothing in his behavior since her arrival had led her to mistake his intentions in that regard. She opened her mouth to assure him of that only to remember she wasn't Rose. It wasn't her place to give him assurances. He'd never been considering a marriage alliance with her.

Natalie looked awkwardly away from him and realized there was one person close enough to overhear them, after all. Rose herself.

Relief swept over her, and she waited for Rose to step in and say something. But Rose seemed frozen in place, her eyes on Leo.

Leo cleared his throat, clearly uncomfortable with the lengthening silence.

"I mean no slight on your personal charm, of course. I know my cousin—" He cut himself off, looking guilty. "What I mean to say, is that it's not about you personally at all. I know that as crown prince, my duty is to my kingdom, and I intend to dedicate my life to Lanover. But I cannot love where I am instructed to do so. I refuse to even attempt it. Love shouldn't be about cold-blooded gain."

His words hit a little too close to home, and Natalie winced. She couldn't let him keep talking, telling her his private thoughts on the matter because he believed her to be someone else—someone of his own rank who understood the burdens of royal life.

She threw Rose an apologetic look. She had wanted to talk to her first, but at least they were both there.

"Please stop, Prince Leo." She stepped away from him, holding up her hand between them.

He stepped after her, looking worried. "I truly mean no offense."

"None is taken," she said swiftly. "At least by me. However, you might feel some offense when you hear the truth. So please bear in mind that I also meant no offense. Neither of us did."

"Us?" He looked strangely relieved. "Are you talking of Luca?"

"Luca?" Natalie was momentarily distracted. "No. Why would I be—?" She shook her head. She needed to focus. It was time that everyone knew the truth.

"I'm talking about Princess Rose and me."

He frowned. "I don't understand. You are Princess Rose."

She drew a deep breath. "Actually, I'm not. I'm Natalie. And she's me. I mean—" She winced at the tangle of words. "I mean that the girl you know as Natalie is the real Princess Rose."

"Posey is Princess Rose?" His face was devoid of all expression, as if he was working hard to conceal his true feelings.

Now Natalie was confused. "Posey?"

"That's what Natalie said she preferred to be called...I mean....Rose said?"

They were both lost in the confusing mash of exchanged identities.

"You're serious?" he asked, still carefully blank. "The

companion who arrived in Lanover with you is the true Princess Rose?"

"Yes, Your Highness. I'm very sorry for deceiving you. We only intended to do it for a few days as a…game of sorts, and meaning no disrespect to you or the Lanoverian court. But then—"

She looked over at Rose, her eyes pleading for help. Leo's brows contracted, and he turned, following her gaze.

As soon as his eyes met Rose's, she unfroze. But instead of coming to Natalie's rescue, she turned and fled further into the garden.

"No, wait!" Natalie called. "It isn't—"

Leo didn't hesitate, running after Rose without a backward glance for Natalie.

"—safe," she finished, more quietly. Clearly neither of them was listening to her, but at least Rose wasn't on her own.

What had just happened? She wasn't sure, but Leo hadn't exactly looked angry as he chased after the princess. So hopefully that meant there wasn't going to be an international incident?

She sighed and turned back toward the ballroom. At least now she could stop avoiding Luca. He might even be able to shed some light on his cousin's odd response.

Her gaze swept idly over the garden as she turned, skimming over the gardener who was unobtrusively working to clear party debris from the lantern-lit sections of the garden. Her eyes continued on to the ballroom before her mind caught up.

She recognized that face!

She swung back around to find the gardener had straightened and was looking toward her. Their eyes locked.

Her attacker.

# CHAPTER 16

"Don't try running away again!" a commanding voice ordered from behind her.

Natalie didn't turn to look at Luca, her eyes still locked on the man dressed as a gardener. He had started to back slowly away, still watching her.

"I don't know why you're avoiding me." Luca's voice came closer. "I thought we were past all that. If you can dance with Leo, surely you can take pity on me and dance with me too."

She still didn't turn, her mind racing as she tried to decide what to do.

"Lila?" Luca sounded less sure. "Have I done something to upset you?"

The fake gardener dropped the pretense and ran. Natalie shifted her weight, about to dash after him, but Luca's presence held her back, like an anchor.

She had once told Luca that if she needed his help, she would ask for it. She had failed that test the first time, overconfident in her own abilities. She wasn't going to make the same mistake again.

Natalie was the only one who knew the man's features, but in Lanover she was on Luca's home turf, not her own. He had proven himself several times over, and it was past time for her to stop shutting him out. They needed to do what they should have done from the beginning and work as a team.

"Luca." She met his eyes, a wealth of meaning in her own. There wasn't time for speeches, just one important sentence. "Will you help me?"

His eyes lit up, his earlier worries wiped away. "Always."

"Then run!" she cried already sprinting in the direction the gardener had fled.

Luca wasn't far behind, quickly closing the distance between them.

"What is it?" he asked as he drew level with her. "Where are we going?"

"I saw him!" she panted. "He was here. Disguised as a gardener. I think he might have been trying to get to Rose."

"Your attacker?" Luca's words were sharp, the exertion not yet leaving him breathless. He increased his pace, pulling ahead of her. "Which direction?"

"Wait!" She caught at his arm, pulling him to a stop as she tried to catch her breath. "I've lost sight of him. I don't know where he's gone." She wanted to scream with frustration.

Unless…

"He was dressed as a gardener," she said quickly. "What if he actually is one? You must have an army of them with a garden this size!"

Luca considered the possibility. "It would explain how he's managed to get the notes into your bedchamber. As a palace gardener, he could have passed them on to an unwitting maid, claiming they were love notes from a courtier. Plenty of the maids would find that appealingly romantic and would do as asked. It would also explain why he chose meeting spots inside the palace grounds. That's been bothering me."

"In that case," Natalie said urgently, "he may have fled to the gardeners' quarters. He may even have the stolen documents and seal there. He'll want to fetch them before he flees the palace completely. If we're fast, we can still catch him. Where do the gardeners stay?"

"By the orchard." Luca started running again, calling over his shoulder. "Follow me!"

He led her toward the orchard and the building that shielded it. As they neared it, he slowed, his eyes searching the area.

"Whenever the royal family throws a ball at the palace, they also fund festivities throughout the city. Most of the palace servants go into the city to attend one or other of the events there, so I wouldn't expect too many to be here."

"That should work in our favor," Natalie gasped, once more fighting for breath.

"If he's here, he's already inside," Luca said. "You should wait out here while I go look."

Natalie shook her head firmly. "I'm the one who knows what he looks like, remember? We're doing this together."

Luca glanced at her once, his mouth twisting down, but he seemed to recognize the futility in protesting.

"Besides," she added, "we don't know he's in the

building for sure. Are you going to leave me out here alone and unprotected?"

She looked at him with wide, innocent eyes, and he chuckled.

"Point taken. But you can't blame me for wanting to keep you safely away from him. You have no idea how horrifying it was to hear your scream last night. I'd nearly given up on that section of the gardens, and I keep thinking about what would have happened if I'd moved on even a few minutes earlier." He shuddered. "I was awake for hours thinking about it."

Her heart softened. "But I'm perfectly all right because you did save me. And I'll be even safer once we have that man in custody." She hesitated, glancing back toward the main palace. "But I don't want him to hurt you either. Maybe we should fetch some guards before we go any further?"

"If we leave now, we risk losing him entirely." Luca examined her carefully. "If you're afraid, we don't have to do this. I can escort you back to the ball immediately. But I know I won't rest easy while he's still at large, and this might be our only chance to catch him. Now that he knows you've recognized him, he won't stay long."

Natalie shook her head. "He's gotten away too many times already. I'm not letting him slip through our fingers again."

Luca nodded and drew his sword. "Stay behind me."

Natalie took a step back, more than happy to acquiesce with any safety measures that didn't involve her staying behind. Luca moved to the main door and tried it. It opened easily, giving them access to the shared residence.

The large communal room on the other side of the door looked as if it served a variety of purposes. It currently sat empty, however.

Luca led the way toward a corridor that gave access to the rest of the building. "Individual rooms must be down here," he said. "But they'll be locked. I don't like the idea of breaking down the door of every gardener in the palace. But I didn't think it would be this deserted. If we can't find anyone to ask, I don't know what else to try…"

They entered the corridor, and Natalie tried the closest door. As expected, it was locked. She turned to say as much to Luca and caught a flicker of movement.

"There!" She pointed down the corridor.

A door near the far end had opened, and her attacker stood frozen, half out of his room, his eyes fixed on them.

"It's him!" she yelled.

The man threw a glance back over his shoulder but must have realized his room was a dead end. The lock wouldn't hold long against their concerted efforts.

Throwing his small bag over his shoulder, he ran for the large window at the end of the corridor. They dashed after him, but he was much closer and managed to unlatch it and swing it open before they were halfway there. Pushing his bag through the opening, he slithered through after it.

Natalie lengthened her stride, but a loud crash made Luca slide to a stop, his arm flying out to hold Natalie back as the crash of falling glass died away.

She peered over his arm at the stone on the passageway floor between them and the window, shards of glass all around it.

"Was he trying to hit us?" she asked. "He wasn't even close."

"No," Luca said grimly. "He was doing that to the window." She followed the line of his pointing finger and saw a gaping hole in the middle of the window, surrounded by jagged shards of glass still attached to the frame. "He's making sure we can't follow that way."

# CHAPTER 17

Luca turned and sprinted back the way they'd come, clearly expecting Natalie to follow. But he'd have to go back through the main room and then circle the whole building before he could get a clear line of sight to the fleeing man. The blackmailer could be gone by then.

Glass splintered beneath her boots as she ran in the opposite direction, across the shards now littering the corridor floor. She could at least track him through the window until Luca appeared.

But when she reached the end of the corridor, another idea struck her. She didn't need to go through the broken pane itself. If she pulled the window all the way open, as her attacker had done, she should be able to slide out without running afoul of the shards still inside the frame.

A door opened halfway down the corridor. "What's going on?" a sleepy voice asked.

Natalie turned to see a man peering in her direction,

blinking in confusion. At least one of the gardeners had chosen to catch up on sleep rather than go out to celebrate.

"Help me!" Natalie gasped. "I need you to hold this window open while I climb through."

The man stepped all the way into the corridor, his eyes widening in alarm. "Now, look here! You don't want to go doing that. There's broken glass everywhere!"

"I can see that," Natalie cried, already turning back to see how far the blackmailer had gotten. "Now hurry! Hurry!" She said the final word so forcibly that the man rushed forward.

He took the window frame from her and held it open as far as it would stretch. She hoisted herself up on the ledge and slid carefully through the opening, shrinking herself down as much as possible and taking care not to even brush against the jagged edges of glass.

"Thank you!" she cried as she tipped out the other side, only just catching herself with her hands as her legs slid through. There had barely been enough space, but she'd made it.

"Go fetch some guards!" she called to her assistant as she leaped to her feet, her eyes already looking toward the last place she'd seen the fleeing man.

Movement at the end of a row of bare orange trees caught her eye. He was fleeing north along the far end of the rows.

She didn't bother chasing him up the aisle of trees. She didn't want to catch him, just keep track of his location. Running along the closer end of the rows, she kept pace with him, straining to match his speed as he flashed past the end of each row.

"Luca!" she screamed as she ran. "Over here!"

She didn't dare look back to see if Luca was close. All her attention was on keeping track of her quarry in the moonlight and making sure he hadn't disappeared between one row and the next.

When he did pivot, turning down one of the aisles between two rows of trees, she nearly missed it. It took her several strides to slow down and turn, and when she did, he popped out of the trees in front of her.

They dove for each other at the same time. Her attacker seemed to have realized she was temporarily alone and had decided to go on the offensive. Natalie, however, was determined to hold him until Luca arrived.

Her opponent managed to seize one of her arms, but she used her momentum to spin, pulling him around with her and breaking herself free. Twisting sideways, she clamped her arms around his knees and brought him crashing to the ground.

He swore, pushing himself into a sitting position and scrabbling for the knife at his belt. Natalie let go and scrambled backward, as if she were one of the crabs Luca had shown her on the beach.

"Lila!" Luca finally arrived, lunging the last of the distance and pressing his sword tip to the man's throat.

Her attacker went still, hatred in his eyes as he glared up at the prince. Luca didn't take his steely-eyed gaze from the man.

"There's a pile of orange picking bags over there," he said to Natalie. "If you detach one of the straps, we can use it to secure his hands."

Natalie raced to obey, removing the strap and bringing it back.

"Do you know how to tie a secure knot?" Luca asked.

She grinned. "Of course I do. I'm not really a princess, remember? I know how to do all sorts of practical things."

She bound the man quickly, pulling the knots extra tight despite his protests. After his attempt to murder her, she had no sympathy for his discomfort.

Luca prodded the man to his feet, pointing him in the direction of the main palace. The man grunted, his eyes darting in every direction, but no one appeared out of the darkness to save him.

Natalie retrieved the bag he had been carrying which he had dropped in the scuffle. As she trailed behind the other two, she rummaged through it. There was no sign of any documents, but at the bottom she found a small leather pouch.

"Aha!" she cried, pulling it out with joy. "I think I've found—Yes! It's the missing Arcadian seal. It matches the one used on my letters."

"That's not mine," the man said quickly. "Someone must have put it there. I don't even know why you were chasing me."

Natalie rolled her eyes. "Don't bother trying that. I recognize you from that time you tried to murder me. Remember that occasion?"

Luca gave him a threatening jab with his sword, the prince's expression turning savage at her mention of the murder attempt, and the man subsided.

They made it most of the way to the main palace

building before they met Natalie's gardener assistant, who was hurrying back in their direction at the head of a squad of confused guards. A shout went up as the men caught sight of Luca and his prisoner, and the guards all broke into a run.

The captain of the squad stopped at Luca's side, giving Natalie a chance to quietly pocket the pouch with the seal. Two other guards converged on the prisoner, seizing him roughly from either side. When yet another guard stopped respectfully in front of her, she handed him the blackmailer's bag. She hadn't noticed anything else of interest inside, but there might be something to establish the man's identity.

The bulk of the squad marched the prisoner away, but the captain hesitated, looking between Luca and Natalie.

"Are you sure neither of you have been harmed, Your Highness?" he asked. "The princess must be very shaken. We can provide an escort to see her safely back to her maids."

"I'll take her back to her room myself," Luca said. "Please ensure the prisoner is held securely."

"Of course, Your Highness." The man bowed once in Luca's direction and a second time toward Natalie before hurrying away with the last of his men.

Natalie stepped closer to Luca. "I kept the seal," she said quietly. "I'll return it to Rose directly."

He nodded his approval. "We should be able to keep the Arcadian aspect of the situation out of any official proceedings. His attempt to murder you will be a sufficient charge to bring against him."

Natalie sighed with relief that the whole ordeal was over. Despite all her mistakes, she had helped bring down the blackmailer in the end. They'd even recovered the stolen seal.

A horrible thought occurred to her—one she should have considered from the beginning.

"But what use has he made of the seal in all this time?" she asked. "If he used the documents he stole as a guide, he could have created any number of falsified papers by now! What should we do?"

"Nothing," said Luca firmly.

She stared at him, bewildered.

"That man tried to murder you in our palace grounds. There was no way I was letting him wander free. I'm very pleased that we've also recovered the missing seal in the process, but that—and any documents it created—are an Arcadian matter. And, as you just recently pointed out, you are not, in fact, an Arcadian princess." He grinned at her. "But it so happens that we do have an Arcadian princess in our midst. So I suggest we leave the question of any missing documents to her to sort out."

"But surely we should help her!"

Luca was unmoved. "If Princess Rose needs help, I think Crown Prince Leo would be a more appropriate person for her to apply to than either of us—wouldn't you agree?"

Natalie considered the matter. "Yes," she said decisively. "You're quite right."

She had overestimated her own capability quite enough lately. She was more than happy to leave the retrieving of any documents up to a prince and princess who had the resources of two kingdoms behind them—not to mention Aurora's spy network.

"You don't need to worry," she told Luca. "I've finished overstepping in all areas. I won't meddle with finding the documents, and your cousin is safe from me, too." She shook her head. "I've always thought that if you want something, you should make it happen. I couldn't understand why other people didn't do the same. But I was so busy thinking about how I wanted to be a queen, that I never stopped to consider if I'd be a good queen."

She gave a wry chuckle. "I think it's fairly clear after the last few weeks that no one should be entrusting any kingdoms to my care."

"To be fair," Luca said, amusement in his voice, "you are only eighteen. There aren't many eighteen-year-olds who would be good at ruling a kingdom. Even Leo—who was raised for the role—has told Uncle Frederic that he isn't allowed to retire for at least thirty years."

"The worst of it," Natalie said in a defeated voice, "is that I don't think I'd even like being royal, after all. All those tedious court occasions and the endless small talk. Being on display all the time…" She sighed. "Gwen is going to laugh at me. She tried to warn me that I might not like being a queen as much as I imagined."

She looked wistfully around the garden. "I will miss Lanover when I leave, though. I'd convinced myself it was my future home, and it's just as beautiful as I imagined."

"You're leaving?" Luca sounded dismayed. "You're not just giving up on being queen but leaving Lanover completely?"

"Of course. I never had any true claim on your family's

hospitality, so I can hardly stay and continue inflicting myself where I was never invited. Rose will be returning home in a week, and I'm hoping she'll let me travel as far as Arcadia with her. That's assuming she'll still speak to me after I blurted out the truth to Leo."

Luca raised his eyebrows. "You told Leo? How did he take it?"

Natalie shrugged. "I have no idea. He dashed off almost immediately."

Luca frowned, but after a moment he shook his head, apparently dismissing his cousin's strange behavior from his thoughts.

A cool breeze hit Natalie's bare arms and shoulders, and she shivered. Now that the excitement of the chase was past, the cold of the night was seeping into her.

"Thank you for helping me," she said. "And for not taking offense at our charade. I hope that one day Lanover will become just as close an ally of the mountain kingdom as it is of Arcadia."

"I think," Luca said with an enigmatic smile, "that there's a good chance of that."

Natalie tried to feel pleased at the prospect, but all emotion seemed to have leached out of her along with the heat of the chase.

"Goodbye," she said. The word felt utterly insufficient, but she couldn't think what else to say. She began walking toward the palace.

"This isn't goodbye!" Luca said quickly. "You said you're not leaving for a week."

She stopped and turned back with a sad smile. "But as

of now, I'm no longer Princess Rose of Arcadia. So I'm certainly not going to push myself into court gatherings any longer. I think I've already done quite enough of that."

"Lila!" he called after her, but she kept walking, and he must have thought better of it because he let her go.

$\mathcal{N}$atalie's feet tried to take the familiar route back to her room, but the room she'd been occupying wasn't hers anymore. In truth, it never had been.

She turned in another direction, walking to the room Rose had been using instead. Joanne leaped up when she entered, looking disappointed to see it was only Natalie.

"Where's Princess Rose?" she asked, abandoning her sewing on her chair. "Didn't you see her at the ball? Is something wrong?"

Natalie, overcome with sudden exhaustion, shook her head. "No, it's nothing like that. She's probably still at the ball. But I'm tired and wanted to come to bed."

"But why are you here, then?" Joanne asked.

Natalie stared at her, remembering only slowly that the maids didn't know the charade was over. After everything that had happened, Natalie's confession to Leo seemed like a distant memory. But it had actually been less than an hour since she'd spoken to the crown prince.

"We've told the princes the truth," she said in a flat voice.

"So it's time for us to swap back to our proper places."

"Thank goodness for that," Joanne said tartly, rushing to pack up her sewing. "It's been quite long enough—and more too, if you ask me."

"Yes," Natalie said, still fighting against exhaustion. "You're probably right."

Joanne paused in her work and peered at Natalie. "Are you all right, Miss?"

Natalie summoned a smile. "Yes. I just need to sleep. If the others are still awake, maybe they could help you swap back all our belongings. Rose should be in her rightful room now."

"They'll be happy to help," Joanne assured her, rushing out of the room to go find the other maids.

Natalie sighed. She hadn't meant for Joanne to leave quite so quickly. She was desperate to slip straight into the bed, but she couldn't unfasten her ball gown without help. She would have to wait for the maid's return.

Joanne returned with all three of the others, each of them laden down with bags and gowns. Natalie raised her brows as they made equally short work of gathering up Rose's belongings. Clearly the maids had been impatient with the ruse for some time. Perhaps since the very beginning.

"Could you help me?" she asked Cate meekly before the maid could slip back out the door, and Cate stopped with a startled exclamation.

"Oh yes, of course! You can't sleep in that!" She laughed at her own joke.

She made short work of the gown's fastenings before wishing Natalie goodnight and vacating the room, leaving Natalie completely alone. Natalie gave a long, grateful sigh and locked her door. She had never been so grateful for solitude.

She swayed with tiredness as she changed into her nightgown, desperate to escape into sleep. But as soon as she was lying down, the exhaustion lifted. She tossed and turned, unable to sleep as her mind raced over everything that had happened in the last two days.

Eventually she got back up and feverishly packed all the belongings the maids had carried over loose. She couldn't remain in Lanover for another week, after all. She would find a way to start back home the next day.

The frenzied activity—or perhaps the decision to leave in the morning—settled her enough that when she fell into bed again, she was finally able to fall into sleep as well. She would have a proper conversation with Rose in the morning—she owed the princess that and more—and then she would leave the capital completely. Everyone would be more comfortable that way.

The sound of insistent knocking woke her in the morning. She had intended to search out Rose, but the princess had already come to her.

"Just a moment," she called groggily, looking around for her dressing gown and realizing it had fallen prey to her frenzied packing the night before.

"Take your time," called back a cheerful voice that did not belong to Rose. "I can wait out here all day if need be."

Natalie froze. What was Luca doing at her door so early in the morning?

She had intended to say a formal goodbye to him and Prince Leo before she left, of course, but she hadn't expected to see him like this—alone and in her nightgown.

She gasped. She couldn't see him in her nightgown!

In an even more frenzied rush than the night before, she undid all her work, pulling items out of her bags at random, searching for a simple outfit that she could manage on her own. When she was dressed, she pulled a brush through her hair so roughly that she winced, her scalp still tender.

Sweeping the hair up into a loose arrangement, she focused on making it secure rather than neat. She sighed at her reflection as she pushed in the final pin. Hardly a charming picture, but at least she was respectable.

She unlocked the door and inched it open, preparing herself for the disappointment of an empty corridor after keeping the prince waiting so long. But Luca was still there, leaning against a wall, one leg propped up and his hands in his pockets, the picture of unhurried ease.

He smiled so warmly at the sight of her that her heart leaped in her chest, her pulse pounding in her throat.

"What are you doing here?" she asked. "How did you even know where to find me?"

He pushed off the wall and came to stand in front of her, holding out his hand as if they had just met, his gaze commanding. Bewildered, she put her hand into his, and he bowed over it, his lips lingering against her bare skin.

She gasped softly, pulling her hand away as fire raced up her arm. How could he still affect her so intensely, even after everything that she'd done to ruin things?

"I heard Princess Rose brought a friend with her," Luca

said while she stared at him. "A girl from the mountain kingdom. She sounded so intriguing that I wanted to come and introduce myself. I haven't met many people from the mountain kingdom. And, of course, as a prince of Lanover, I should welcome all guests to our palace."

"Luca," she said, "what are you talking ab—"

He cut off her words, still with that same warm smile on his face and laughter in his eyes.

"I've heard your name is Natalie. But you prefer to go by Lila? Allow me to introduce myself. I'm Prince Luca of Lanover. But don't be fooled by my title. I'm a very minor and totally inconsequential royal, several steps removed from the line of succession. You can hardly consider me a royal at all."

"Luca!" she cried in protest, but she was laughing now.

"I'm certainly not the kind of prince who would scare away someone who's decided she doesn't want to be royal," he said. "Just in case you happen to know anyone like that."

"Just in case," Natalie said, trying to be grave and failing.

"It's amazing how often people overlook a second prince," Luca continued airily. "They barely notice me at all."

Natalie looked at his broad shoulders and the angular, beautiful lines of his face. "Somehow I don't believe that," she murmured.

"I barely even attend royal functions," he added.

"Just the odd one or two?" she suggested, and he inclined his head.

"Perhaps one or two here and there. Just to keep things interesting, of course."

"In between orange picking," she said, and he brightened.

"I see you understand it perfectly."

He took a step closer and slid his arms around her waist. She didn't pull away.

"So," he continued, leaning down and whispering the words into the hair near her ear, "if, one day, a beautiful young woman from far-off lands wanted to rethink her stance on becoming a princess, she would find me a very adaptable sort of prince."

Natalie shivered, delight uncoiling inside her and spreading from fingertip to fingertip. She slid her arms around his neck and stood on tiptoe to murmur in his ear.

"I think I can give the matter serious consideration."

His mouth traveled along her jawline as he dropped featherlight kisses against her skin. "Let me help with your deliberations," he breathed, reaching her mouth and pressing his lips to hers.

She pulled him closer, kissing him with abandon, not caring who might walk past and see.

She had no desire to be a queen any longer, but she just might see her way clear to becoming a princess one day. As long as Luca was her prince.

To discover the parallel story of Princess Rose as she experiences life as a commoner, read To Entangle a Heart: An Entwined Prince and the Pauper Retelling.

Or if you missed first meeting Natalie as she helps stage a rebellion, read the two books in the Four Kingdoms duology now available in a single volume, To Ride the Wind and Steal the Sun.

To be informed of my new releases, as well as new bonus shorts, please sign up to my mailing list at www. melaniecellier.com. At my website, you'll also find an array of free extra content in my Four Kingdoms world.

Thank you for taking the time to read my book. I hope you enjoyed it. If you did, please spread the word! You could start by leaving a review on Amazon or Goodreads or Facebook or any other social media site. Your review would be very much appreciated and would make a big difference!

# ACKNOWLEDGMENTS

*To Ensnare a Prince* marks ten years since my first publication—which happened to be *The Princess Companion*, the first book in my Four Kingdoms world. I'm so grateful to the readers who have been journeying with the Four Kingdoms for a decade now. They are the ones who have made these books possible, and I continue to be touched by their kind words, their stories, and their love for these books and characters. Thank you all so much! You mean so much to me. Whenever I hear about families connecting over my books, or people finding an oasis in the pages in the midst of anxiety or stress, it gives me more reasons to keep writing.

And as I reflect back on a decade of publishing, I'm equally grateful for the team who support each of my books with so much care and dedication. I've said it in so many acknowledgments now, but my gratitude only grows.

To Lyra, Karri, Mary, my parents, Deborah, Rachel, Greg, Adrian, Priya, James, Rebecca, and Esther—thank you for the integral part you play in bringing each of these books from idea to publication. And thank you for your patience with me.

And thank you to God who gives me the ultimate

reason to stay on this journey through all the ups and downs—the knowledge that good will, in the end, vanquish evil. And that, at the end of the day, love truly is the most important thing.

# ABOUT THE AUTHOR

Melanie Cellier grew up on a staple diet of books, books and more books. And although she got older, she never stopped loving children's and young adult novels.

She always wanted to write one herself, but it took three careers and three different continents before she actually managed it.

She now feels incredibly fortunate to spend her time writing from her home in Adelaide, Australia where she keeps an eye out for koalas in her backyard. Her staple diet hasn't changed much, although she's added choc mint Rooibos tea and Chicken Crimpies to the list.

She writes young adult fantasy including books in her *Spoken Mage* world, her *Mage's Influence* world, and her various *Four Kingdoms* and *Kingdoms of Legacy* series that are made up of linked stand-alone stories that retell classic fairy tales.

www.ingramcontent.com/pod-product-compliance
Lightning Source LLC
Chambersburg PA
CBHW051702180726
48283CB00004B/1179